Of the Book

Corners of the World, Volume 1

Madness Heart Press

D1518250

Published by Madness Heart Press, 2019.

Madness Heart Press
2006 Idlewilde Run Dr.
Austin, Texas 78744

This is a work of fiction. Names, characters, places, and incidents either are the product of the author's imagination or are used fictitiously. Any resemblance to actual persons, living or dead, events, or locales is entirely coincidental.

First Edition December 2019
Cover by John Baltisberger
www.madnessheart.press

Table of Contents

The Shadeem

Lorraine Schein

Though there are no Jewish fairies,
there are magical beings
called the Shadeem or Mazikeen
who are like the Arabian Jinn.

The Talmud says that the Shadeem were the offspring of Adam—
after he had eaten from the Tree of Life,
he was excommunicated for one hundred and thirty years
during which he lay with spirits, demons, and spectres of the
night,
and begat the Shadeem.

The Shadeem are said to resemble angels in three ways:
they can see but not be seen;
they have wings and can fly;
they know the future.

In three ways, they resemble mankind:
they eat and drink;
they can marry and have children;
they are subject to death.

Like the Jinn,
they have the power of shapeshifting.

During the Holocaust,
the Shadeem knew where the transport trains were going,
knew what the smoke coming from the factories was.

Some flew away;
some became invisible,
pushing the guards off the trains to their deaths.
Others assumed the shape of Nazis soldiers,
saving Jews selected for the grave.

The Shadeem warned the children,
who sensed what they were,
and escaped with them
borne away in their arms,
flying over the death camps
stacked with ash piles from the ovens.

The children were flown to the forest,
where they lived with the Shadeem for a while,
before being given to a kind human couple.

After the war,
the Shadeem told the children
what they had seen
and smote old Nazis in their dreams.

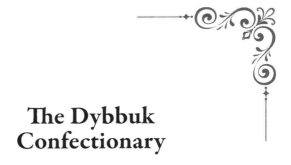

The Dybbuk Confectionary

Eliza Master

YOU WEAR A WHITE TAFFETA flower on your head just like Billie Holliday. The wind is grabby on the way to the theatre. It's the old mean kind that yanks your umbrella inside out. The gusts tangle your hair and push coarse strands between your lips.

A small river has formed over the trolley tracks. You risk a few raindrops on your coat and close the umbrella to use it as a crutch. Getting your French leather shoes stained and ruined would be a tragedy. So, you point your toes like a dancer and leap. The umbrella slips away from under you.

You land in the flood. You are doused. Shame on that dirty Philadelphia rain! You reach for the flower clip in your hair, to set it straight. And you push up on the wet elbow, determined not to be late.

Out of nowhere, a trolley is barreling toward you at high speed. You make eye contact with the driver. He stands and waves at you frantically. But your head is filled with the clattering of the trolley wheels. You hear screeching metal and smell burning. There is a gush of wind, and the vehicle knocks you down into the stream. It rides across you, crushing your breast. There is a flash of pain that sears like a lightning bolt. You don't breathe. The bones break in your neck like a shattered teacup. Your heart pumps twice and once more before the blood empties on its own. And then you feel better.

You watch the driver drag the handsome girl from under the trolley. Her head skitters along in its own rhythm, still attached to her neck by a few tendrils. You see that her face is clean, though bloodless, and the white flower is still where it should be. You see that she is you. People pick you up and bring you back home. There is no Jewish morgue in Philadelphia, so they lay you on the dinner table.

Your mother is sobbing. "Candy, Candy, my beautiful girl, how did this happen?" You hate that your name is Candy, but you don't have a voice to tell her. She puts a rag across your neck to hide the mess, and gently swabs off your blouse.

Benjamin pulls on her apron. "Is she dead, mommy? Is she going to heaven, mommy?" Your mother cries louder, and your brother matches her tenor. "Mommy, Mommy, Mommy!"

Soon Father comes home. He waits till Mother is gone to the latrine before choking out his own tears. He rests his forehead against what's left of your chest. His skullcap slips off. Then he lifts his head, bellowing, "Why God!" You think that the whole block can hear him. Mother comes running with Benjamin in her arms. You are sad and sorry, and you miss being alive. Mother makes a bed of pillows, and all three spend the night on the dining room floor with your body.

Obeying Jewish law, they bury you at Mikveh Israel the following afternoon. A wood board marks your grave. It reads,

Candy Newberg, Born 1920, Died 1935. The soft dirt muffles the world above, and you are exhausted. So, you rest with your body underground. Which is precisely what you are doing when you hear a verse that awakens you.

Candle shining with flame enchanted.
By magic may my wish be granted,
Dybbuk ghost of Candy I call,
Into my box, you shall fall
The dybbuk mold you make
Will be mine to take....

You don't want to leave the safe coffin, but the spell is so alluring you can't resist. You rise through the fresh earth and see the Dybbuk Catcher. He holds a lit red candle in one hand and an empty matchbox in the other. His brow pinches, and his eyes squint as he repeats the sugary rhyme. You fight the draw, but it overcomes you, and you climb into his box. He seals the edges with melted wax, leaving only a pinhole of early morning light. You are trapped.

You bob along the road in the Dybbuk Catcher's pocket. Shortly you feel him push open a door and recognize the entry bell of Crain's Confectionary. You have enjoyed their buttercreams and rich sipping chocolate many times.

"Morning, Mr. Crain," says a gal as you pass. You imagine her bonnet and embroidered apron, and wish you were she. Mr. Crain bounces you up two flights of stairs and sets your box on a shelf in the corner of the room. Through the pinhole, you see a wall of drawers. One drawer is labeled, Body parts; Foot, and another reads, People; Supernatural Witch.

"Daddy, Daddy!" A boy climbs up the stairs lugging a toy goat with four wheels. His cherry cheeks and pooh bear eyes shine as he rides the animal across the chocolate room. While petting the goat's fur, he accidentally drives over his father's shoe.

"Boy! You don't belong here!" shouts the Dybbuk Catcher angrily. He sticks out his leg and topples goat and the boy. The toy goat's head pops off its wooden neck and rolls under the table. You remember that is what happened to your head as well. Fervently, the boy goes after the goat's head and kisses its furry face.

Meanwhile, Mr. Crain plops your box into an open drawer, along with two slabs of unblemished lead. It is midway up the wall. You can feel other dybbuks trapped in the drawers surrounding you. They smell like horse manure and whisper old Yiddish. Their discontent itches in your soul.

The Dybbuk spell from the graveyard does its work. You feel a great lurch in the bottom of your being. Then- Presto! Your soul has made a mold. There is a loud plunk, and both Mr. Crain and the boy stare at your drawer. You have etched a design into the lead slabs. It is a rendition of a goat on a boy.

You realize all the drawers are filled with molds made by Dybbuk souls. Now you understand why Crain's is praised as the most original and inventive confectionary in Pennsylvania. Certainly, Hershey's can't compete with the intricacies of a Dybbuk mind.

Mr. Crain marches over to your drawer. "By God!" he exclaims. You see that his grave digger face is transformed by a wide smile. "Son, this one is for you."

The child trots over. "Goat's is better?" He reaches out a hand to pet the mold.

Mr. Crain sashays over to the copper melter, brimming with molten chocolate. The boy trails after him. You feel proud as he fills the mold and places it on the marble table for cooling.

"Is it done, is it done?" asks the boy impatiently.

"No, sit!" commands his father. "I will come back when it's ready. Don't move." He points to a lonely chair with its back to the room. You feel sorry for the little one. The Dybbuk Catcher stomps down the stairs.

Naturally, the boy jumps out of the chair and rushes to the warm mold. With tiny fingers, he pries it open while humming a familiar song.

"Candle shining with flame enchanted.
By magic may my wish be granted,
Dybbuk ghost of...."

Here the child pauses, not sure what comes next. The mold pops apart and luscious chocolate spills onto the table. A bright smile lights up his face. He shouts, *"Candy!"* and finishes the spell with your name.

You whisk out of the matchbox and burst out of the drawer to land on the boy's shoulder. He laughs with abandon as though he can feel you. The melted chocolate is all over his face. The buttons of his vest are smudged. No one notices that Mr. Crain has returned.

"Bad boy!" Mr. Crain smacks his son across the cheek, leaving a bright red blemish. You have never hated anyone as much as you hate the Dybbuk Catcher. He hauls his son downstairs.

You fly out the window. And you keep flying. You leave Philadelphia, and you fly around the world. You go to the chocolate plantations in Africa and the confectionaries in Paris. Melted chocolate smells like freedom.

Eventually, you return to Crain's confectionary. Above the door is an illustration of your mold, goat and boy. Inside, the melter is on, saturating the air with rich chocolate. You see that the boy has grown into a steady gentleman. His tawny hair has turned silver. You remember your drawer and fly upstairs to see that it is ajar and empty. The other drawers are empty too, and the room is quiet. The dybbuks have gone away.

And the Dybbuk Catcher is gone, too.

High Culture

Yael Levy

"ENJOY THE CULTURE," Eli says, strapping the baby into his car seat, as the kids clamor into our huge, gray minivan. I sit in the front seat, adjusting my long-sleeved shirt on a hot August day.

"You make it sound so simple," I say, as I hide my Star of David necklace under my collar.

"Isn't it?"

"I've been planning on attending this literary festival in Decatur for months. And you tell me today about the Torah party?"

"So go. Enjoy your novelists. The high culture."

"Don't guilt me."

Eli lets out a sigh as he starts the ignition. "How often does a scribe finish the yearlong process of writing a new Torah scroll? Such painstaking work—copying a Torah with quill and ink onto dried parchment—exactly as our ancestors have done since the times of Moses."

"I go to shul. I pay yeshiva tuition. I try to be kind. And I never, ever get to go to a literary festival. Never get to experience high culture."

Eli drives steadily through the lush green streets of Atlanta. "Maybe even before Moses. Maybe Abraham wrote on parchment with a quill."

"I'm a soccer-mom-aspiring-writer whose best literary friend lives miles away. You made us leave New York—now I have no network."

"So network. I'll pick you up when we're done celebrating our ancient culture," Eli says, as he drops our son Izzy and me off in Decatur.

I try to hold Izzy's hand to cross the street toward Decatur Square, but he shrugs it off. A huge poster of Anne Frank—stands in the square, advertising a Holocaust exhibit at the Town Center. Anne stares at me, her dark eyes round like a Seder plate, the sweetness of a rich heritage mixed with marror—the bitter herbs of thousands of years of exile and pain.

A chill runs down my spine. Anne resembles my own daughter, Sarah. Sarah, who's dancing now, celebrating the birth of a new Torah scroll.

"Your Sarah could be Anne's twin," a Holocaust survivor had once told me. She'd been a neighbor of Anne's back in the Old Country, before... Sarah, who's probably snacking on crackers and drinking soda even though I tell her the chemicals aren't good for her acne.

"Would you like to join our writers' group?" A fellow calls out to me, as he hands me a pamphlet and adjusts his Burberry sunglasses.

He is tall and beautiful. His hair is light blond, the color of lemonade on a sunny summer's day. His features are perfect, straight aquiline nose, square jaw, even teeth. He is dressed in a white Abercrombie T-shirt, white chinos I saw advertised from Banana Republic.

Finally, a fellow writer—tribesman.

He hands me a pamphlet, and I scan it, feeling the gaze of Anne Frank on my shoulders. He takes off his glasses, and I look into his eyes. They are empty.

I look away. I'm afraid. Why are his eyes empty? If times got tough—What would he do?

"C'mon Ma," Izzy tugs my sleeve.

The writer blinks.

"Uh, later," I say, and let Izzy drag me to a booth showcasing tomes of ancient idols and a golden Pharaoh. Izzy begs me to buy a book about ancient Egypt.

"I suppose we could place those next to our Haggadas—and commemorate our slavery in Egypt?" I shrug. We walk until we reach the romance writers. Are my tribesmen here?

"How y'all doing?" A chubby woman with curly brown hair wearing a low-cut tank top sits at a makeshift table at a booth, signing autographs as if in assembly line.

Her hair frizzled from the humidity; sweat drops down her neck like a waterfall to the deep valley between her large bosoms.

"Did you write this?" I ask, pointing to a stack of paperbacks on the table.

"Sure did," she smiles, flashing a huge set of canines, sharp like fangs.

I blink and look again. Her fangs are gone, leaving only somewhat uneven teeth.

"It's hot," Izzy whines, "Can we get a drink?"

"I could use one too," the lady winks, "Yeah, this is my series. I write erotic Halfling romances."

"Halflings?"

"Yeah, you know, half man/ half beast."

Izzy interrupts us. "This is boring. We should've gone to the Torah party."

Other women behind me, push their books to the author for her autograph.

"How do they look these half men/ half beasts?" Do they have empty eyes?

"They look exactly like you and me." She smiles at me, her fangs sharp and white in the sunlight.

I rub my neck, feeling the Star of David weigh heavily on its chain.

"And these Halflings—they fall in love?"

The author laughs, as the women keep lining up. "It's that alpha male thing, y'know. Only instead of behaving like a wolf—my heroes are wolves. And vampires, and shapeshifters."

Women behind me laugh. "Very hot," one woman hoots.

"Sexy," another whispers in agreement.

I turn around to look at the women. They are all dressed like well-heeled southern ladies. Their hair coiffed, their dresses and skirts pressed. They look respectable.

I gulp.

One woman is smiling, her fangs sharp as she fans herself with a paper fan. A fellow behind her peruses the authors' books and absently twitches his ears—sharp, pointy on top of his head.

Another woman has the feet of a wolf. She knocks some of the author's books off of the table with her tail.

I bend down to pick up the books.

"Did you say you're a writer?" the author asks, "Care to join us?" I turn to face her.

The air is still.

I look around and see nobody familiar. Most of my tribe is at shul, celebrating the birth of a new Torah.

"I'm a writer," I stutter, "But don't recall having told you that."

I suddenly feel very afraid.

If cultured Halflings or men with empty eyes attacked me, my son— we'd have zero chance of survival. There'd be nowhere to hide.

The hair on my back is raised high like a hunted animal when I feel the predatory circling of Halflings closing in around us. I grab Izzy's hand and run.

We run past the booths and gazebos where chunky old ladies are spinning yarns as old as time. We pass children, authors, and happy couples meandering through the fair. We rush past vendors hawking freshly made lemonade and concessions selling baked pretzels and peanuts and fried green tomatoes.

We flee past good Southern folk—as well as Halflings and men with empty eyes.

We reach the square, panting.

The square. Perfect location to be herded, shot, eaten or...

I look up at Anne.

She is smiling.

Her dark eyes round like a Seder plate, the sweetness of a rich heritage mixed with marror—the bitter herbs of thousands of years of exile and pain.

"There's Daddy," Izzy points to our minivan, idling outside the square.

I clutch Izzy's hand, and run to the van.

Izzy lets me hold his hand.

Through the open car window, I hear the kids squabbling, singing. Jewish music is blaring from the CD. Sarah is bopping up and down, dancing to the music. "You missed it, Ma! It was so fun! The dancing! The food! Everyone together—it felt so alive!"

I adjust my Star of David necklace and place it outside of my collar.

"Did you enjoy the high culture?" Eli asks as he unlocks the door for me.

"You bet," I say, and slam the door.

As we drive away, I peek through the rear-view mirror and watch the man with empty eyes welcome bystanders to his tribe. He stands solidly in the square beside the huge poster of Anne Frank, his eyes shielded from the sun.

Rabbi Aaron meets
Satan

Tim Lieder

RABBI AARON LIVES ON the moon of Alpha Centauri Six, studying and teaching Torah every evening to a small congregation. He runs a butcher shop by day. His charts mark the time of Shabbat on Earth, but sometimes he flirts with using the Alpha Centauri Moon cycle with its 18 hour days, and it's 128 day years. The Beis Din on Alpha Centauri Six has debated adopting the 19-year cycle from earth to other planets for decades.

Rabbi Aaron's neighbors come to his store with sheilahs. Many times he feels unworthy. He rarely hears from earth or the ACG Beis Din. His people had to learn to make their own food and sew their own clothes. Rabbi Aaron is worried because he's alone. His wife died, and his children made Aaliyah decades ago.

Rabbi Aaron's neighbors are losing their hold on reality. They see great calamity approaching in visions and dreams. They are arming themselves. They even peruse the dead texts of the Karaites and haskala for guidance.

Rabbi Aaron wonders if they might be right. He tries to avoid lashon hara, but he doubts David VII, or David 7.05b as the union insisted. David VII is a machine, an artificial intelligence with knowledge of Torah, Talmud, Halachos, and Kabala with thousands of commentaries for every situation. A computer can calculate the changeover in times from earth to Alpha Centauri and even give several acceptable rulings to the Jerusalem dilemma. Rabbi Aaron worries for himself and his people. He has studied the time of the Universal Monotheists when Jews suffered under the forgotten pagans that worshipped Baal, Asherot, Christ, and Mahomet. Jews that strayed from Torah had created monsters. The misunderstanding between a student and his rabbi killed millions over 3000 years.

Lost in thought, the rabbi doesn't see the pale man standing above him. The man speaks, and Rabbi Aaron smells cinnamon perfume. The man laughs.

"Why are you laughing?"

"You are such a serious rabbi. History will claim you for a fool."

"What are you doing here, sir?" Rabbi Aaron recognizes the perfume. It belonged to Becky Apollo, a girl from a misnagdim family that proposed inappropriate marriage.

The man searches his pockets for something. He draws out a yoyo, a penknife, and a screwdriver until he settles on a small yellowed parchment.

"Is this your signature?"

Aaron looks at the parchment. An old contract, something he signed in Yeshiva days. He was to bring synthetic cocaine to Alpha Centauri Six. He signed it and threw it in the incinerator.

"Yes. But I did not send it to you."

"You sent it to Heaven, and that's where I found it."

Rabbi Aaron laughs. He has not heard his own laughter for years. It contains a touch of hysteria. If laughter could summon the messiah, Rabbi Aaron would have seen him that evening.

Satan, for that's who he was, stands and watches.

"Thank you, sir. I see that I have much more work before I can call the responsibilities of the world upon myself."

The paper crumbles on the desk.

"I will still tell them about this."

"As you wish."

"Would you like to get a bagel? There's a very nice place on King Street."

"No, thanks. I prefer Yemenite food."

"Suit yourself."

Satan puts a finger to his hat brim and leaves. Rabbi Aaron sings a niggun and says Tehillim all night long.

Ungodliness

David Margolis

YEHUDA POPKIN WAS BORN in the village of Lask, Poland, near the town of Lodz. The year was 1533. His father, Mendel, was a rabbi who was neither brilliant nor charismatic, and the size of his congregation was modest. His mother, Malka, had three children until she died giving birth to Yehuda. The bereft Mendel arranged for his infant son to feed on the left breast of Hannah Ginsburg, their housecleaner, while Hannah's infant daughter, Golda, occupied her right breast. Golda was a vigorous and voracious suckler, and at six months, she was almost twice the size of the rabbi's asthenic son.

Mendel soon found another wife, for even a mediocre rabbi, was held in high esteem by the Jewish community. He married a buxom eighteen-year-old, Luba Cukerman, a daughter of a moneylender. She turned out to be remarkably fecund, and they had six healthy children together. The fertile Luba became the dominant Luba, and eventually, Mendel himself didn't know if he ever had an original thought when it came to his large family and its finances. As a consequence, he buried

21

his nose deeper into the Talmud, trying to decipher Yahweh and his mysterious ways.

The young toddler didn't smile or make eye contact, and he didn't say a word until he was four years old. By then, it was obvious that something was terribly wrong with the boy. The local physicians were of no help, still believing Aristotle's writings that the heart was the seat of intelligence. In those days, every twist and turn of life was attributed to the mercy or the wrath of God, so that the inhabitants of Lask believed that the Almighty had frowned upon Yehuda and his family for reasons unknown, but it was something that prayer had been unable to fix, even the supplications of a rabbinical father. A vicious rumor began to circulate in the community that the boy was occupied by a dybbuk.

As Luba's family multiplied, she was determined to remove Malka's offspring from the household, thus reserving Mendel's meager income for her own children. She married off Malka's two daughters soon after they reached puberty, and an older brother, Chaim, was sent off to study Torah in Krakow. This left only the strange, incoherent Yehuda from the first wife's progeny.

The little boy's behavior became more bizarre as he reached six and seven years of age. He would scream and cry when he couldn't be understood, rocking back and forth and banging his head into walls, doors, and even hot ovens. He was only calm when Hannah came over to clean the Popkin house, bringing Golda with her. The two children would skip rope and ride on an old hobby horse that had once been Mendel's. Golda could decipher Yehuda's shattered language and strange mannerisms, the boy even laughed in her presence, but when

Hannah and Golda returned to their hovel, Yehuda would go back to his temper tantrums: punching, thumping, stomping, and whomping, not to mention wailing, which resulted from the whippings of Luba.

Yehuda was an impossible student. He was expelled from cheder because of his disruptions and his learning disabilities, but partly for his own sake. The other pupils taunted the poor boy mercilessly, taking delight in bloodying his countenance with their fists and their boots. He took to aimlessly roving about the village. Sometimes Kaminski, the shopkeeper, would give him a small piece of chocolate, and the boy might smile, until one day, he caught Yehuda with a whole bag of Kaminsky's candy in his school satchel. At thirteen, Yehuda was just able to write his name and recite a few blessings, not enough to celebrate a Bar Mitzvah. Despite all this, Mendel was a loving parent, and unlike Luba, he never laid a hand on the boy in punishment. During his destructive moods, the rabbi would take him on walks and sing Jewish melodies to him, trying to calm the turmoil in the boy's psyche. Perhaps his black curly hair and pale complexion reminded him of Malka, who in death, evoked the image of Ruth or Esther compared to the dictatorial Luba.

The number of congregants dwindled as stories persisted that Rabbi Popkin was harboring a devil in his household. With his reputation at risk and the synagogue in dire financial straits, the despairing rabbi went along with Luba (did he have a choice?) and agreed to consign Yehuda to a gruff dairyman who took the boy in exchange for the forgiveness of a debt owed to Luba's father.

The farmer treated the boy like a slave. Yehuda was awakened before the sun rose to help with the milking. He was given a bowl of thin gruel before he led the cows and goats to pasture. After that, he swept the barn, after that, he brought the animals back from their grazing, after that, he did some more milking, and after that, he ran away and hid in Lodz where he eked out an existence as a beggar. He wandered the streets, wearing a tallis (prayer shawl) and a yarmulke, begging for a scrap of bread here, a cup of milk there, an occasional egg, or a bowl of chicken soup. He became thinner by the day and gave up speaking completely. He would nod his head and take the crumbs that were given to him. Sometimes he would offer himself to work as a day laborer, cleaning out the stables of the rich men of Lodz. He attended the services on Shabbos and the High Holidays, but he reeked so badly of horse manure that the sexton of the synagogue hid him in a dusty broom closet where he prayed in silence, just barely hearing the chants of the lusty cantor.

One day, while out begging, he fell in behind a wedding party. He couldn't help but notice the bride in her dazzling white wedding gown. As he ran up beside the nuptial wagon, he recognized the bride as Golda, his breast-mate from long ago. He waved his arms, his gaze fixed on her angelic beauty until he stumbled into a pothole, half-filled with muddy rainwater.

When Yehuda was twenty-seven years old, he developed a dry hacking cough, the harbinger of tuberculosis. His meager appetite diminished even further, and he looked like a walking cadaver with a long straggly beard. One cold, snow-blinding day, he sought cover under a bridge and went to sleep. The following spring, as the snow was melting, a peddler noticed a foul odor as he was crossing that span. He notified the authorities, and Yehuda's decomposed body was found wrapped in his tallis. He'd been dead for four months.

It took several weeks for the body to be identified and transported to Lask. He was buried in the family plot next to Malka and the fresh grave of Mendel, who had died a few months previously. The family sat shiva for seven days, and his brother, Chaim, said the daily kaddish prayers for the required eleven months. A year later, a tombstone was unveiled over his grave with an epitaph in Hebrew, He was a Man of God, meant to dispel the notion that he was occupied by a devil.

Yehuda's spirit arrived in Sheol well before his body had been buried. He was so insignificant in life that an apprentice angel, working the night-shift, was assigned to categorize his soul. Boguslaw had seen him coming, but it was almost dawn, and he was just starting in on his breakfast of kippered herring and rye bread smeared with goat cheese. Unlike souls, angels were allowed to eat, and some of these beings had enormous appetites. The poor man was kept waiting in death as he had been in life. Finally, Boguslaw whispered. "Yehuda."

"That is I."

"You've just died, Yehuda."

"I knew I wasn't feeling well but died, you say?"

"Yes, sir. I'm responsible for categorizing your soul and making sure it gets to where it needs to go."

"Well, Heaven, of course. For the torture that I lead on Earth, surely there must be a just reward for me in the afterworld. Isn't that how it works? We suffer on Earth to get payback in eternity."

"Yes, in theory. But nowadays, there's a lot of red tape." Boguslaw remarked.

"Red tape?"

"Rules and laws and proclamations and edicts and decrees, stuff like that. Oh sure, some special ones come through here from time to time, big-shot rabbis, prophets, and rich people. The gentiles, of course, have kings and nobleman, queens and princesses, but I don't deal with them, I'm just here for poor Jewish souls like you. Other than your suffering, there's nothing that makes you qualify for a place in Heaven. No charitable deeds like giving money, food, or shelter to the poor."

"I was the poor. I was a beggar."

"Begging's nothing to brag about. You haven't prayed three times each day or fasted on Yom Kippur."

"I fasted daily. There was never enough to eat."

"That doesn't count." Boguslaw was getting edgy. "But Hell is another matter. You're not substantial enough for that."

"Substantial?"

"Well, you stole that bag of candy from Kaminsky when you were a kid, and then there were the seventeen apples and eight pears that you pilfered from Goldstein's fruit stand over the years. But that's not enough to get you into Hell."

"So where to?"

"You're classified as surplus, a so-so soul, if I could use an alliteration." Boguslaw smiled at his witticism. "You're neither good nor bad. In fact, well over 70% of spirits fall into that category. As the Earth's population has lived and died, there's been overcrowding. We can only store so many souls in Heaven, or Hell, for that matter. You'll become a ghost and wander the Earth until an opening comes up. Eventually, you'll be recycled back into a living thing, could be a human, could be an animal of some sort, but that's above my paygrade."

"And the dybbuk?"

"Don't concern yourself with foolish superstitions. We're here in the real hereafter, no make-believe demons like that." Boguslaw chuckled.

"Wait just one minute, Mr. Angel, what about God?"

"What about Him?"

"What about His mercy, His kindness, and the rewards of one's devotion to the Supreme Being? He must realize there's been a mistake, and I can still get to Heaven for the tortuous life I endured dybbuk or no dybbuk. Yehuda started to chant the sacred words, Shema Yisrael Adonai Eloheinu Adonai Echad. Hear, O Israel, the Lord our God, the Lord is One."

"Unfortunately, God can't hear you right now. He's far away, working on other projects."

"Other projects?"

"The universe is constantly expanding. He has plans for creating new worlds, new heavens and hells, and performing miracles, stuff like that."

"What about here on earth with us Jews, the Chosen People, and all."

"To be honest, he's evaluating other people in other galaxies. He let evil get into this world with that snake in the Garden, and things just got out of hand. Let's face it, the world has gone a bit haywire."

"Haywire?"

"Just look at yourself. Such a poor excuse for a human being."

YEHUDA-SOUL WAS RELEASED into the biosphere. It
had no form, no name, and no need for sustenance or sleep.
It couldn't stop a runaway carriage, save a drowning child, fur-
nish the needy, or minister to the dying. It couldn't even haunt
a house. It traveled in the clouds, but couldn't feel the wind
in its hair or the rain on its back. It didn't make an imprint
in the sand or a ripple on water. Other apparitions passed by,
middling souls like himself, and occasionally, they'd nod their
heads in recognition. There could be fifty or more of these
specters perched on a rock, on a dock, or in a sock. Yehuda-
soul was blown all over the Earth. It viewed Stonehenge before
the Anglo Saxons, visited the Grand Canyon with the Paiute
tribe, and discovered skulls of the Neanderthals who lived before Adam, just another haywire scheme, it guessed.

It spent time hovered over Yehuda's grave. Once or twice,
Chaim came by with his sisters, Bessie and Laika, and they
placed stones on top of his tombstone in the Jewish tradition.
After thirty years, it saw a grave dug, and Luba's body was
dropped in. Fifty years passed. It witnessed Golda's funeral, and
it would have wept if a soul could cry. After seventy-five years,
all its half-brothers and sisters were buried, and after a hundred,
all their offspring were interred too. Eventually, no one even
knew who Yehuda Popkin had ever been, although he hadn't
ever been much. With the passage of time, his name and epitaph were eroded from his tombstone until it was a smooth
gray tablet. Then, the soul stopped visiting. It found solace in
the environs of a northern Manitoba forest and lived quietly in
a spruce tree with the squirrels.

In 1903, it heard a summons and was transported back to Sheol. "Long time no see, Yehuda." It was Boguslaw.

"Exactly 343 years since I've been only just a soul. Nice wings, Bogey, something new?"

"I received my promotion in 1900. It took seventy centuries, but I made it to a full-fledged angel."

"What do you want from me?" asked the soul.

"An opening has come up. We're going to store you for a while, and then send you back to Earth."

"Store me?"

"I've a spot for you, on the fourth block of the fifth row, in the fifteenth section of Heaven."

"Heaven, that's great news!"

"Andy thinks something big is coming down, so we've expanded."

"Andy?"

"Andy runs heaven nowadays."

"Not God and the patriarchs?"

"Andy was promoted from a human to chief angel. Not many have accomplished this feat other than Elijah and Enoch, who were shot right up from Earth in their chariots. You could include Jesus in that group, but that's a story for the Gentiles. Andy's the go-to guy nowadays."

"How did Andy manage that?"

"As a man, he was in advertising, in New York City no less. His birth name was Avraham Abramowitz, but he changed his name to Andy Anderson after he left Poland."

"There was a Rabbi Avraham Abramowitz in Lodz."

"Yes, that would have been his great-great-great-great grandfather. That rabbi's dear soul is in Heaven, in a special space with a spa, and an amphitheater where the spirits pray with the big boys: Abraham, Isaac, Jacob, Moses, Aaron, David, and Joseph. After Andy died, his soul was located in the VIP section as well. Andy befriended Moses, and one day, he pitched his idea for a special addition to Heaven, where souls could be stored more efficiently. Andy had proposed a similar project for mass-producing pre-fabricated homes while working on Madison Ave. Moses talked to Abraham, who talked to Yahweh in outer space. They advanced Andy up the ladder in order to implement his ideas. Now he's in charge of the daily workings of Heaven, you know, like a chief operating officer."

"You learn something new every day," said the soul.

"If you'll just approve these papers, we'll get you situated in your new home. It's a bit cramped, but you'll only be housed there until you're sent back to Earth, less than fifty years, I'd guess."

"How big a space do I have?"

"It's five inches by five inches."

"That's small, even for a ghost. I'm used to living in a tree that's 80 feet tall."

"Ghost, schmost, soon you'll be a man again, ready to conquer the world. Remember Andy's slogan, mighty men from little souls can grow."

YEHUDA-SOUL FOUND ITS little home at the end of a long row in the fifteenth section of Heaven. It keyed in the eighteen-digit number on the door handle. There was a soft click, and the door swung open. Yehuda-soul peered in. There was a miniature blue and white box attached to one wall, a tiny chair, and a small table with a single drawer. Yehuda-soul opened the drawer and found a microscopic scroll. As it unrolled the scroll, a voice in the box began to read. In the beginning, God created the heavens and the Earth. The voice continued to read until all of Genesis had been recited. Yehuda-soul began to feel weary and put the scroll back in the minuscule drawer in the diminutive table. After a while, it opened the scroll again, and like clockwork, the intercom voice started to read. This might have gone on for days or years. It didn't know, there was no way to keep track of time. The soul didn't see the sun or the moon or the stars or the dancing aurora borealis during a Manitoba winter. It just existed.

One day, Yehuda-soul heard a rustling, like a sparrow outside. The pintsized door swung open. A wispy being stood at the threshold. There was a beguiling softness to the ghost that Yehuda-soul remembered from the time it had been a man.

"This is my old apartment. There must be some mistake," said the satiny soul.

"Aren't you Golda?"

"Who?"

"Golda, Golda Ginsburg. I shared your mother's breasts with you when we were infants."

"When was that?"

"In 1533, when we lived in Lask, Poland. You were my playmate."

"I've lived many lives since then, I think five or six. Once I have a new body, I forget the flesh that came before. My last stop was Cincinnati. I was a teacher who taught in an orphanage. I had four wonderful children, and a fine husband, a doctor."

"I've never been human since I was Yehuda in Lask. I saw you on your wedding day, but you didn't recognize me."

"It wasn't to be, I guess."

"I couldn't talk or think properly as a man, and I ended up a beggar. After I died, I was classified as a surplus soul. I traveled the world as a phantom, then I lived in a tree for two hundred years. Now, I guess we'll share this little space. I've been so bored in here all by myself."

"It's different since Andy took over," said Golda. "We used to hold prayer meetings with all the souls. We'd sing and dance. David would play his lyre, and we'd praise God. Now we're packed in here like sardines, and they pipe that canned Bible into each cell. Andy says God's on sabbatical." Golda-soul emitted something like a sardonic laugh.

"Maybe this is God's will. For you to be my soulmate."

"You think?"

And so, they cohabitated in their tiny cell. Yehuda-soul would tell Golda-soul how hard was his life in Lask, and how much he loved her then. Golda described the gentleness of her husband, the delight of sixteen grandchildren, and her work with the orphans. They talked about what their life might be on Earth: the cities they would visit, the food they would eat, the anniversaries they'd share, and the love they would have for each other. Yehuda blushed, if a soul could blush, and told Golda that he'd never had sexual relations with a woman, but Golda told him he'd do just fine. But they never spoke of God, Golda wouldn't allow it. They communicated with Boguslaw and begged him to return them to Earth as a couple. They didn't care if they were rich or poor or where they lived. They knew that life could be hard, even cruel, but anything would be better than a cell five inches by five inches.

It was some twenty years later that Boguslaw spoke to them through the intercom. "I've been talking to Andy, and I've got good news. He thinks he can work things out for the two of you. You'll both be born in Europe next month, Yehuda, in Prague and Golda in Vienna. You'll meet when you're twenty years old." The two souls began to sing the Shema. Yehuda-soul was surprised that Golda was singing.

Then Golda asked, "How did you get Andy to agree? I thought he'd abolished that kind of thing."

"He has, but he apologizes that you two ended up in the same cubicle. That isn't supposed to happen. He'll let you have your fun on Earth, but there is a catch."

"Catch?" asked Yehuda-soul.

"He's not sure how many Jews he'll need in the future. Your next gig could be a new group of humans that he's designing. You might not be Jews the next time around. Andy's always tinkering."

"Where will we meet?" asked Golda-soul.

"In Poland, in Lodz, in the ghetto, in 1942."

"That's where I died as a beggar, Andy's got a sense of the theatrical," said Yehuda-soul. He laughed while wrapping his wisp even tighter around Golda's ethereal tendrils.

"Two years later, you'll travel to your final destination."

"And where would that be?" asked Yehuda-soul.

"I'm not sure he's worked that out yet," said Boguslaw.

Twice Buried

Carolyn Geduld

BREAKING NEWS: TEN elderly hospice victims shot in first nursing home mass killing in U.S. history. Active shooter killed by police.

It was nearing two weeks after the atrocity, the funerals, the investigation, the candlelight vigils, the updates by the police chief and the mayor. For the Berg family, it was the end of the shiva, the Jewish practice of mourning for seven days following a funeral.

The world had moved on. There were other events dominating the news cycle. But Eli Berg was still emerging from the stunning occurrence that ended Grandpa Berg's fragile life, just days before his natural death had been anticipated. Now the family was expected to return to normal activities—Eli to his job at the bank, Sarah to hers at the agency, their seven-year-old daughter, Celia, to second grade.

Grandpa Berg was Eli's grandfather and Celia's great grandfather. At age 97, the elderly man had outlived his son by two years. This was another tragedy in his life. After his son's death, his grandson Eli had moved him to the nursing home. When

Grandpa began to fail, he was transferred to a hospice room. This was the section where he and nine other hospice residents were murdered by the maintenance men, for reasons that remained mysterious.

At the shiva service on the evening after the funeral, the Rabbi made the point that Grandpa Berg, a Holocaust survivor, had been killed twice. As the story had been told many times, Grandpa Berg had been shot by the Nazis in Thereisenstadt and was thought to have died. Miraculously, he recovered and emigrated to America after liberation.

He was known to have been a very quiet man who worked hard and who slept when he was not working. Eli's father had told Eli that his primary childhood memory was being shushed by his mother and driven outside to play in order not awaken his father. Eli's primary childhood memory was of his father being in what he called a "black hole" and of his mother's secret drinking. They were both depressed. Eli had a lonely childhood. He thought marriage would mean never having to be lonely again.

During the funeral, Eli wept on Sarah's shoulder. She was dry-eyed. She had not really known Grandpa Berg. She did not recall ever having had a conversation with the taciturn man. Moreover, her family had come to America in the early 20th Century and had avoided the fate of European Jews. The Holocaust was two generations in the past. Maybe "Never forget" did not have to mean "remember every minute."

Now, his murder was another thing altogether. Ten hospice victims shot to death in a nursing home? That was part of her lived experience. She could relate to the horror of it, the senselessness, the suffering of other families. But in the end, although she would not say it out loud, the victims were about to die anyway. They just died sooner, and—who knows?—maybe in a kinder way than lingering in pain. She thought of her mother, dying of cancer, wanting to be let alone, not fussed over. Her mother would have preferred quick clean death.

In his grief, Eli clung to Sarah, leaning on her, hugging her, repeatedly saying, "Why did this happen" and "If only I had let him stay in our house instead of putting him in a nursing home."

After two days of this, Sarah's patience gave out, and her familiar irritability returned. More and more, she was concluding that the murderer had done her grandfather-in-law a favor. If only Eli could see it that way.

"Eli," she said, "You are right on top of me. I can't move. Just give me an inch, for God's sake."

"I want to be near you," he said. "I'm so... sad, angry. I can't believe Grandpa Berg has been murdered. Murdered! My grandfather!"

"I know. I know," she relented. What could she do? She put her arms around him briefly and patted him on the back. Then she pushed him away with both hands. "I've got to start dinner."

Tears gushed down Eli's cheeks. Celia ran to her father and threw herself at him.

"Don't cry, Daddy," she said. Eli hugged her and wept.

"Eli. No!" Sarah said sharply. "Pull yourself together. Don't make Celia take care of you."

"Okay, okay. You're right," Eli said, extracting himself from Celia.

Celia followed her mother into the kitchen. Like her father, she asked repetitive questions, to Sarah's annoyance. But Sarah dutifully answered the child, knowing that the murder confused her and possibly frightened her. Yes, Grandpa Berg was dead. Yes, he was buried in the ground. Yes, he would turn into a skeleton.

Celia went to her room and turned on her iPad. She played her favorite cartoon, the Three Bears. Goldilocks had to choose which bowl of porridge to eat. Porridge was the same thing as oatmeal. If she chose Papa Bear's, the porridge was too hot. It could burn your tongue. If she chose Mama Bear's, the porridge was too cold. Cold porridge was yucky. If Baby Bear's, it was just right.

Celia wondered why the Papa Bear porridge was different from the Mama Bear porridge.

Just then, Sarah was remembering how she met Eli. A few months before meeting him, she had broken off a relationship with a married man who would not leave his wife for her, despite many assurances. The affair had lasted for two years. Then the wife found out, and her lover phoned her in his wife's presence. He told her he loved his wife and would not see Sarah anymore.

Sarah had been devastated. After weeks of weeping and beating her pillow with her bare fists until they were raw, she finally accepted the inevitable and "moved on," as all her friends advised. What no one knew was that she was never to completely forget her married lover and the horrible humiliation of his rejection.

Then Eli, who had been a friendly presence at Friday night services in the Reform synagogue, began to sit next to her. He asked her for a date. He was Jewish. He was not married. She accepted.

Eli was a perfect boyfriend. He was attentive, considerate, affectionate, and punctual. She couldn't complain. He gave her small gifts and texted her several times a day during work hours. He was a good conversationalist. They shared the same political views about both America and Israel. They both wanted a family, at least one child, maybe two.

Sarah felt that Eli's devotion was healing after her previous lover's neglect and broken promises. She wasn't exactly in love with him, but she no longer believed in being "in love." Where had that got her? She accepted Eli's proposal. They were married in the synagogue.

After they were married, they moved in together. That was when Sarah realized that perfection in a boyfriend was not necessarily perfection in a husband. The attentiveness Sarah enjoyed two or three times a week was not as pleasing on a daily, minute-by-minute basis. Whenever they were together, they were together. Eli wanted to be in the same room, not more than three feet away, touching her as often as possible, talking to her, at her, staring at her, breathing in her scent.

At first, Sarah was polite and gentle.

"Darling," she would say, "Could you move back a little? You are making me hot."

Or, "Sweetheart. Don't sit so close. My arm is cramping."

Eli would apologize and oblige. Bur a short time later, he would be right next to her again, with a hand on her knee or across her shoulders, his warm breath on her cheek, constricting her, smothering her.

Over time, her tone became sharper. "Eli. Too close. Move back. Give me room."

At her agency, she had warm feelings for her homeless clients. At the same time, her supervisors stressed boundaries. The staff was not to have personal relationships with the clients. They were not to give them money or invite them into their homes. Closeness with clients ended at the front door. But with her husband, closeness began at the front door. Sarah figured that God must have created skin to keep people from twining around each other's organs and bones, the way some cancerous tumors do.

When the subject of boundaries came up, what Eli said was:

"What boundaries? I love you, Sarah. I just want to be with you. What's wrong with that?"

Sarah did not have an answer. Something was wrong with it. She didn't know what. Sometimes she thought that her marriage was a slow-motion chase. Wherever she went in the house, whether for a purpose or just to have a few minutes with her own thoughts, Eli was at her heels. Sarah despaired.

After Eli had moved Grandpa Berg to the nursing home, a discovery was made hidden in Grandpa's old room. It was a tiny diary, with minute Yiddish handwriting on scraps of crumbling paper. They were remnants of his time in Thereisanstat, preserved at great risk and hidden, even in America.

Eli sent the original to the Holocaust Museum in Washington D.C. In return, the Museum sent Eli a copy. He immediately put it in his desk drawer, unread. Sarah, on the other hand, did look at it from time to time. Because her grandparents spoke Yiddish, she was able to translate. After Grandpa

Berg's murder, she took it out and opened it randomly to one of the tiny pages:

"Di situatsye iz leyt. es iz keyn hofenung."

"The situation is dire. There is no hope."

Sarah stared at the sentences, rereading them several times. Something about them hit her hard. For the first time, she really could imagine Grandpa Berg as a young boy, a teen just a few years older than Celia, in the camp, plagued with hunger and disease and lack of privacy, shot by the guards, thrown into a mass grave. Then, in the nursing home, shot again, and buried a second time. There was a hard lump in her chest.

"There is no hope."

The image of being buried took hold of Sarah. She imagined herself shot and thrown into a hole. Dirt shoveled over her filled her nose and mouth. She tried to brush it away, but it quickly covered her, crushing her, depriving her of air. She could not shake the thought.

That night, when Eli returned from work, she was still in the grip of the image. She was in the kitchen, preparing dinner without paying much attention to what she was doing. After taking off his coat, Eli went into the kitchen as usual to help her. When she saw him, her hands began to tremble. The knife she was holding slipped, and a bubble of blood welled up on her thumb.

"Oh, no," Eli said, grabbing her arm, "You cut yourself. Let me see."

"It's nothing!" She said, pulling her arm away as the blood streamed down toward her wrist.

Eli grabbed at her arm again. "Let me see that. It looks bad," he said.

Suddenly, Sarah was screaming."Get out! Get out! Leave me alone. I'll deal with it. Just leave."

Eli lunged for her arm again. "Don't be silly, Sarah. You're hurt."

Sarah picked up the knife and pointed it at Eli.

"If you don't leave the room right now," she growled, "I will stab you with this knife."

"Sarah!" he said, "I'm not leaving."

"Yes, you are," she said, thrusting the knife at him.

"What's wrong with you?"

"I swear, I will stab you with this knife. I swear on the Torah, I will. Get out now!"

"Okay. Okay," he said, reluctantly backing out the door.

Once he was out of the kitchen, she could hear him telling Celia to go to her room and play with her Barbies. Celia asked why, saying she wanted to be with Mommy. Mommy wasn't feeling well, Eli was saying. Celia should wait for Mommy in her room.

Sarah held her hand up and saw that the blood was running down to her elbow. She did not try to stop it by wrapping it with a dishtowel. She watched herself bleed with fascination. Her skin had been broken.

"There is no hope."

Breathing, hard, she put the knife down. The lump in her chest was moving up into her throat. Before she understood what she was doing, she found herself calling for her husband, who she had just chased away.

"Eli! Eli!" She howled.

In seconds, he was beside her with a first aid kit. He bandaged her hand.

"There," he said. He held her close. Celia ran in, shouting "Group hug," and clasped both adults as high as she could reach.

Back in her room, Celia played watched another video on her iPad. This one was The Three Little Pigs.

She liked it when the wolf said: "I'll huff and I'll puff, and I'll blow your house down."

The two pigs whose houses had been blown down ran into the house of the pig who built his house of bricks. Celia thought that the smart pig must have felt very crowded when the other two pigs came to live with him. She wondered if that made the smart pig get angry or sick.

The next day, Sarah and Eli pretended nothing had happened. But Sarah was more irritated by Eli than ever, although she did not yell at him. She did not understand what was happening to her. She even found herself thinking of her old lover. From time to time, over the years, she had driven by his house, hoping to catch a glimpse of him, hoping he would be outside and see her in her car.

Now, on impulse, she told Eli she was going shopping.

"We'll go with you," he said, standing up.

"No!" she said. "You stay here with Celia. Make sure she does her homework."

She raced out the door before he could follow. She drove to her former lover's house. Turning off the car lights, she parked across the street. This was the first time she did not just drive by. The blinds were drawn in the house, but she could see that lights were on in one downstairs room and one upstairs room. Maybe he would sense she was out there, waiting. Maybe he would open the front door to see who had parked across the street. Maybe he would come to her.

After a half-hour, she realized that nothing was going to happen, and she'd better get to the store and back home before Eli called the police to report her a missing person. She had no doubt that he would really do that, especially following Grandpa Berg's murder. For Eli, the vulnerability of his family was now as real as it must have been for his grandfather after Thereisanstadt.

For the next week, guilt about deceiving Eli caused her to be more patient with him. Gritting her teeth, she allowed him to hover over her and ask questions about almost every thing she did. It seemed to her that he was even more closely observant of her than he usual. He called it being interested in her.

"Why are you staring out the window? Is there something out there?" He asked.

She knew he meant why wasn't she looking at him, making eye contact.

"I don't know. I just am," she said.

"Tell me what you are seeing. I want to see it, too."

"Nothing, in particular."

"Let me see," Celia said, joining in. "I want to see."

Eli picked her up so she could see out.

"What do you see?" He said to her.

"Tress. Grass. Sky," she said, pointing.

This was ridiculous, Sarah thought.

Everything about family life left Sarah feeling guilty and inadequate. Why couldn't she enjoy it more? She had a loving, attentive husband—what so many of her girlfriends wished for. They complained of absent husbands who were preoccupied with business, golf, sports, or video games and who never had deep conversations with them. And Celia was a delightful, good-natured child. Why was it so hard to withstand her constant questions and jabber? Why did Sarah long for escape?

The truth was that Sarah was at her wit's end. She thought she would go crazy. More and more, her thoughts drifted to her former lover.

Celia was asking, yet again, "Is Grandpa Berg still dead?"

"Yes," Sarah answered, knowing where this was going.

"Is he still in the coffin in the ground?"

"Yes, he is."

"Is the bad man who killed him in the ground, too?"

"That's right. The bad man is dead, too. And in the ground."

"If you and Daddy die, will you be in coffins in the ground, too?"

"Yes, but not for a long, long time."

Celia considered.

"When you and Daddy die, you and the bad man and Grandpa Berg will all be together in the ground," she said. "Maybe next to each other."

Sarah did not respond. Her thoughts were drifting away from her child. She was distracted by thoughts of her former lover. If she sent him a text—just one text to say hello—would he answer? Did he ever think of her?

For the next few days, Sarah contemplated the idea of texting her lover. She bounced between shame and desire. How could she think of doing something so despicable—and how could she not?

Eli did not fail to notice that his wife was not completely present. He redoubled his efforts to know her, to know her mind as well as he knew her body. Anything she did to elude him made him desperate, just as he was when he was a boy, and his mother was drunk.

He made up his mind that he would wring the secrets out of Sarah until there was nothing left that he did not know. He was finished being gentle. He would use pliers to force her head open if he had to. She would not withhold anything from him, not the tiniest thought.

"What are you thinking?" He demanded.

"Nothing."

"There is no such as not thinking. You were thinking about something. Tell me what," he said.

"I don't know what I was thinking. Nothing in particular."

Eli moved closer, into Sarah's space.

"You are far away these days. If there is a problem, I need to know."

"For God's sake, Eli. I'm entitled to some privacy. We both are."

"I don't need privacy from you, Sarah. You are my wife. There is nothing I wouldn't tell you. Including stray thoughts."

"Don't I know it," she said. Looking him straight in the eye for once, she said, "How many times do we have to go over this, Eli? Marriage is not supposed to be a kind of slavery where you own me, where you are even entitled to my thoughts. Whatever happened to consent, huh? If I can't consent, I'm nothing but your slave. And I don't consent to you knowing my thoughts."

Eli inched closer. "Okay. If we don't consent to knowing each other's thoughts, then it is not a marriage. In marriage, consent is freely given. There are no secrets. That's the point of marriage. It is the ultimate freedom because we do consent to know each other completely. Completely, Sarah."

Sarah raised her voice. "If that is what marriage is, I don't want it!"

Eli flushed. "What are you saying?"

At that moment, Celia walked in.

"I'm hungry," she said.

"I'm saying that if you don't back off and leave me the fuck alone, I don't want this marriage anymore," Sarah said.

Celia took a spoon and banged it on the table. "I'm hungry. I want something to eat."

"Are you saying you want a divorce," Eli said, "Just because I want you to talk to me? Is that what you are saying?"

"I suppose that is what I am saying," she said. "You don't want me just to talk to you. You want to crawl down my throat, and I can't take it anymore. There. I'm talking to you."

"You know what? You are an unnatural woman, that's what. An unnatural human being. You want to leave because I love you, and you can't take it."

"I can take love. What I can't take is obsession."

Celia decided that she would make a peanut butter sandwich. The peanut butter was in the pantry. She pulled a chair inside and climbed on it. She could see the peanut butter on an upper shelf. She would have to stand on her tippy toes to reach it.

"You have always been distant from me from day one. Why is that, Sarah? Has there been someone else? I've always suspected."

"That's crazy," she said.

"Is it that married guy you were with before me? The one who wouldn't leave his wife for you? How often did you actually see him in two years? A dozen times? That must have been perfect for you, Sarah. An unavailable man who never really wanted to know you. A twelve-night stand. That's all he was."

"Shut up. Shut up," Sarah screamed. "You know nothing about it. I hate you, Eli."

Sarah's scream morphed into a loud crashing sound coming from the pantry. There they found their daughter buried under the contents of several shelves—boxes, jars, bottles, many shattered. Celia was shrieking. Eli and Sarah couldn't tell blood from tomato sauce. What they understood at the moment was that their little girl was hurt.

Later in the emergency room, they were told that she was not seriously injured after all. Just bruised. They were able to take her right home. But Child Protective Services would have to be informed. It was routine when a child was bruised.

This was highly embarrassing for Eli and Sarah. They would have to admit they had been fighting instead of paying attention to their daughter. They would be obliged to say that divorce had been mentioned in front of her. There were ugly words said that Celia overheard and might never forget.

After the interview, Sarah whispered to herself:

"Di situatsye iz leyt. es iz keyn hofenung.

Back at home, Celia watched another video on her iPad. It was a Bible story called the Tower of Babel. It was about people who wanted to build a tower high enough to reach God. But God did not want people to get that close. Then God made everyone speak a different language so nobody could tell anybody how to build the tower.

After that, no one could understand anyone.

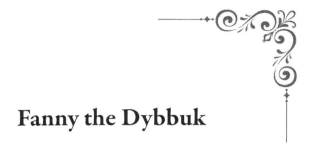

Fanny the Dybbuk

Eliza Master

THE NEW YORK STREETS were dark that morning. Brooklyn was far away from Broadway Avenue, which was lit with brilliant electric bulbs until daybreak. The musty air from winter heating settled between the row houses. Fanny stepped carefully to avoid the mounds of horse manure. She turned her nose away from the grime that street sweepers had swept into piles. Her destination was Hershal's Bakehouse, where she had making bagels, bialys, and bobkahs for the last six months.

On the way, Fanny paused at the haberdashery window to look at her reflection. The window held a perfect picture of the brownstone across the street. The sky was filled with white cotton balls from Brooklyn's smelting factory. But Fanny only saw herself in the glass.

She inspected her gold silk stockings, black shoes, and pretty frock. Her reflection wasn't tall or slim. But she had a womanly figure even though she was only fifteen. Fanny smiled devilishly and unbuttoned the top two buttons on the front of her dress, revealing her brassiere. Quickly she refastened them. She straightened the seam along the back of her right stocking and tightened the garter clip.

Fanny worked with Ruben Hershal, the son of the Bakeshop owners. He was handsome in his clean white skullcap. His young beard made him look older than eighteen. Fanny felt a jolt every time she looked into his long brown eyes, so instead, she would watch his beautiful hands. His graceful fingers were like ballet dancers, perfectly shaping each bread. Last night he reached for her hands even though they were covered with bagel dough. Ruben said, "I love you Fanny." Her name from Ruben's lips sounded American and new, like it never had sounded before.

Fanny was lovesick the next morning when she arrived at the bakeshop and let herself in. She put on the electric light bulb and swept the floor, humming Here Comes the Bride. She stacked wood under the big vat of water for boiling for the bagels. Then Fanny loaded the fire shelf with logs to heat the large baking oven. A splinter scratched her wrist. She hoped the Hershals would get a modern gas oven soon.

Fanny opened the oven door to give the inside a quick sweep. In the back was an abandoned baking tray. The oven floor was barely warm, so Fanny slipped off her shoes and reached into the deep stove. She grasped the tray, but it was wedged between two bricks and stuck. Fanny crawled further into the oven, balancing on her right knee, keeping her left leg raised to hold the door ajar. Yanking the tray, Fanny tumbled onto her elbows. Her left stocking caught on the bottom of the iron door, and her garter unhooked. The lovely gold silk stocking grabbed and pulled the door shut as it slipped off her calf. The iron latch clicked closed. It was a terrible sound.

Fanny was trapped inside the dark oven. She kicked at the door with her bare feet, but it would not open. Fanny's dress was smoking. Flames roared, dwarfing her screams. Then tears poured out, only to be scorched away. She knew the oven would be her grave. Submitting, Fanny flipped onto her back, letting death in. Her passing was eclipsed by the memory of Ruben's soft lips, saying, "I love you, Fanny."

"FANNY? FANNY? FANNY!" called Ruben from the door. The bakeshop was warm with a strange smell. A gold stocking was hanging out of the closed bagel oven. Ruben pulled off the stocking and quickly hefted open the iron door. Inside was his love, Fanny. Ruben grabbed Fanny's charred legs and pulled. Her legs came out easily into the frightened man's hands. Using the hot pole, the rest of Fanny came out in burnt pieces. Ruben wailed. He sat paralyzed in the corner of the baking room. He picked up the stocking from the burnt pile of remains and used it to soak up his tears.

"Meshuganah, meshuganah, meshuganah,'" said Ruben's father when he saw what was left of Fanny. Ruben was still weeping into the stocking.

Soon the whole neighborhood congregated at the bakeshop. Downpours of tears were shed about the loss of such a promising girl. Fanny's father gathered her remains into an old flour bag and took them for burial.

FANNY'S SPIRIT WATCHED Ruben from above as he tried to save her from the oven. She loved him ferociously and wanted to be with him. If only she was still alive! He was wringing Fanny's stocking with his beautiful hands and crying into it. Fanny flew into the stocking and sopped up Ruben's tears.

After a few moments, Fanny's spirit heard the Bakeshop door open. It was Ruben's father. Then her parents came. Fanny wanted to talk to them, but she couldn't. Her ghost was stuck in the stocking. Fanny remembered the stories about dybbuks her grandmother had told her. She said they were unhappy spirits bound to the living world. Grandma's dybbuks wandered around, causing trouble. They were never satisfied. Fanny hoped she wasn't a dybbuk and vowed never to make Ruben's life difficult.

Ruben kept the stocking with him for several months. He carried it in his pocket with Fanny's spirit bound to it. Fanny could feel Ruben from inside the pocket. His leg was warm, and he smelled like yeast. She loved him deeply and hoped she would be alive again soon.

Then one day, the stocking fell onto the bakery floor. Before anyone noticed, Ruben stashed it in an empty baking soda can. He buried it in the storage room under an old bagel boiler.

Fanny was trapped. Fanny smelled the warmth of bread baking From inside the baking soda can. She heard children's voices. Years flowed by. Then, Fanny the dybbuk, heard the croaky voice of an old man. She knew it was her love, Rueben. After that, everything went quiet for some time.

A SONG BUZZED AGAINST the soda can. Fanny tried to understand what the words, Let it Be, meant. Every morning there was more music. She began to look forward to the new songs that vibrated her metal can. Soon bouncy footsteps wandered into the storage room. Someone picked up the dybbuk can and pulled back the lid. Fanny could see! She saw a young man with wispy blond hair. He saw the antique gold silk stocking and took a liking to it. He tied it around his wrist into a soft bracelet.

Fanny looked around the shop from the man's wrist. The only sign of Ruben was a graying photo of him as an old man. It was hanging crooked in the baking room. Fanny missed Ruben and his bagels. She would have cried real tears if she could. Meanwhile, the blond man was forming doughy bialys. His fingers were thin and pale. Then Fanny went home with him.

"Dylan," Said a woman at the door. She had a tight smile and frizzy black hair.

"Hi Mom," Dylan said back, giving her a small hug. Then he went up to his room. Fanny watched him play music on a spinning machine. He rolled up something like tea into a white stick and smoked it. The cigarette and the music excited her. Fanny had been in that soda can for a long time. Being with Dylan made her smile.

Fanny was there when Dylan sang along to Lucy in the Sky with Diamonds. She wished she could join in. He was wearing tie-dye and doing yoga. Fanny favored Dylan's friend George, who was bearishly handsome. Dylan and George swallowed a blotter of LSD. George liked tickling Dylan's wrist under the dybbuk stocking. Then they made love. Fanny liked it very much. Soon Dylan had more love encounters with Rodger, John, and Howard. Dylan's lovers were tender to the stocking and Fanny. She forgot all about Ruben and her former human life. Fanny wanted to stay on Dylan's wrist forever.

But that was not to be. One morning in the bagel shop, Dylan was crying turtle tears. Fanny didn't know what the problem was and she couldn't speak. She tried to sooth Dylan from his wrist, but nothing seemed to happen.

As if he could feel Fanny, Dylan tore off the dybbuk stocking. He balled it up and stuck it into a hole where a wood knot had once been in the ceiling of the baking room. Fanny was stuffed into the insulation.

Again she was trapped. She could hear, but couldn't see a thing. She heard Dylan from the ceiling for a while, like she had heard Ruben. And then everything went quiet again. Fanny the dybbuk, dreamed of her lovers for many years.

NOISE WOKE FANNY UP. People were walking around the bakeshop. Churning sounds with buzzers filled the air. It got warm and then cold in the ceiling. A loud conversation was going on.

"So is everything here really gluten-free?" said a woman's voice.

"Yes, everything. It's for our daughter. And we don't miss wheat at all. Not with so much to choose from." Said another female voice.

"Sorry for the mess, were redoing the place." The second voice went on.

At first, Fanny didn't know what gluten meant. In her dybbuk mind, she thought it might be a beast or perhaps another type of dybbuk. She was glad they didn't know about her in the ceiling all this time. She listened all day and heard the word gluten many times. Fanny learned that it was a different kind of flour.

That night, louder noise came. The bakery shook, and what remained of the stocking shifted in the ceiling. Fanny could see out! Below her was a man installing cabinets. His electric drill made Fanny's dybbuk head ache. Finally, he left, slamming the door hard. Most of the decaying stocking, with Fanny in it, fell out of the ceiling. It was like a small hairball.

From the floor, Fanny saw the morning light streaming through a crack under the bakery door. She heard a key turn in the lock. The door opened.

"Oh, Emily, look at our new cabinets!" A woman announced to the girl with her. She continued, "It will be your job on Saturdays to wipe down the counters and put on all the lights."

"Ok, mom," Said the girl. She had a pointy nose and chestnut hair. Her black pants were clingy and tight. She wore a shirt with the word, 'Rad' on it. Fanny had no idea what 'Rad' meant.

The girl marched towards Fanny and stepped right on the hairball. Fanny was startled and jumped off the hairball right into the girl. The jumping in was an accident. Fanny tried to get out of the girl and jump back into the hairball, but she couldn't. She was cleaved to Emily.

Emily was scared of boys and couldn't eat real bagels or bialys. She spent most of her time reading books. Fanny was bored. She missed Ruben and his bagels. She missed Dylan and making love with George.

Fanny could persuade Emily to do some things. She pushed Emily to secretly buy donuts after school. Emily threw up and got a rash. Without knowing why, Emily decided to eat nothing at all and became anorexic. Ellie's parents were very worried. They sent their daughter to doctors and psychiatrists, but they were no help at all.

A few weeks later, Emily's family went to a Passover meal at Aunt Sylvia's. The matzo balls were light and delicious, just like the ones Fanny's mother had made long ago. And of course, they had gluten. Fanny made Emily sneak into the kitchen to eat one. Just as Emily was about to bite into the matzo ball, the prying eyes of Sylvia saw Fanny. No one had ever seen her as a dybbuk before, and Fanny was scared. She hid deep inside Emily for the rest of the meal.

Sylvia told her sister, Emily's mother, about Fanny the dybbuk. Aunt Sylvia had heard of a rabbi that specialized in this kind of thing. She scribbled down his number and pushed it into her sister's hand.

Emily's mother called the next morning. The De-Dybbuking fee was seven hundred and seventy-seven dollars and seventy-seven cents. The rabbi sounded very confident and was willing to do it that evening at the bakery.

The bakery was closed and quiet when the rabbi knocked on the door. Emily's parents led him to the baking table where they had put out some special gluten-free bagels.

"Please help yourself," said Emily's mother. Sitting with his knees wide, the rabbi bit into the bagel. He seemed surprised at the taste but said nothing.

Fanny wouldn't let Emily eat her gluten-free bagel. She crawled up into the girl's mouth to make her say, "I want a real one." Just then, Fanny saw the rabbi peering at her. She peered back at him from inside Emily. He had a dirty beard and sharp blue eyes. The rabbi was thick around the middle. Fanny heard him breathing. He smiled at Fanny, and she saw his yellow teeth.

"Please shut off the lights," said the rabbi abruptly. He got up and walked under the spot in the ceiling where Dylan had stuffed in the stocking long ago. There was a single strand of golden silk there, hanging down. The rabbi reached above his head and pulled out the strand. He swallowed it in one gulp.

"Fanny." The rabbi said out loud as the thread went down his gullet. The dybbuk uncleaved from Emily.

"I'm better, mommy," said Emily, letting out a big sigh. Emily's parents didn't know if they should believe her. But their daughter was smiling. Perhaps this was what she needed, they thought.

"Thank you very much," said Emily's father as he shook the rabbi's hand. Emily skipped out the door, not missing Fanny one bit.

FANNY WAS IN THE BODY of the rabbi. She went down his throat, clinging onto the silk stocking thread. Below, the rabbi's stomach rumbled. A gluten-free bagel bite was there floating in liquid like a life raft. Using the thread, Fanny lowered herself onto the morsel. Stomach acid was dissolving its edges.

Then she heard music. Was that klezmer? Fanny climbed back up the silk thread into the esophagus. She tore through its membrane only to be confronted with a bracket of tight capillaries. The music was getting louder. She rushed forward towards the sweet melody. There were old-growth veins blocking Fanny's passage, but she fought her way through.

Finally, a clearing opened. Fanny saw the old rabbi's heart. It was flaming and snapping like a campfire. Some dybukks were lounging on ligaments around it. The dybbuks were old with papery skin. One man was reading a book, and another was playing the fiddle. A woman was dancing.

"Oy." Said the fiddle player, as he set down the instrument. His eyes twinkled playfully at Fanny.

"Welcome," said the old man, closing his book. The dancer produced four gold-rimmed wine glasses and filled them with something red.

The dybbuks raised their glasses, and Fanny raised hers too. "L'Chaim, To Life!" they cheered. Fanny drank in the sweet red spirit and warmed herself against the rabbi's heart. Then she asked the old ones, "Is this end?"

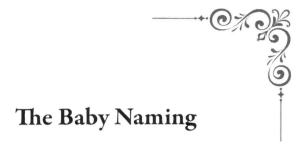

The Baby Naming

Hadley Scherz-Schindler

TOBY WISHED HE WOULD have worn short sleeves. October should not have been that hot. At least his niece's baby naming was on a Sunday, so he did not have to miss any work. His sister, Tamar, was the rabbi officiating this very casual baby naming in his brother's home. Tamar had given him a list of items to procure.

"Why?" he asked her that Friday.

"Nan married into this family, so she doesn't understand," said Tamar over the phone. "And Adam is oblivious. He doesn't believe in the curse."

"I'm not really sure that I do either," replied Toby. Like a responsible oldest child, though, he had gone to the herb store and the Judaica store before it closed on Friday to get sage, frankincense, myrrh, cardamom, a gold anklet for the baby, and a hamsa for the wall. When he arrived at his brother's apartment on Sunday morning an hour before everyone else, his little brother, Adam, took the bag from him and gave him a big hug.

"Thanks, man," Adam said. "Tamar's been bugging me all week about getting this stuff. I can barely keep my eyes open."

"Sure," said Toby.

"Adam?" called his wife, Nan, from the other room. "Is somebody here already? No one's supposed to come for another hour?" She sounded panicked. Nan had not showered in three days. Adam was supposed to make sure she had at least fifteen minutes to shower and dress to look presentable.

"Don't worry," said Adam. "It's only Toby. He's here to help." Adam knew this would relax Nan because Toby was like a brother to her, too. Adam had to travel a lot for his job, so Toby had been her emergency contact throughout the pregnancy. He had come over in the middle of the night when a tree fell on their roof when Adam was in Toronto.

Toby could hear the baby crying in the next room and then silence.

"Hey, you've been here five minutes and haven't asked to see the baby!" remarked Adam as he poured a cup of coffee for Toby. Toby accepted the coffee and handed over the bag of items he'd brought.

"Yeah," said Toby. "I love my niece, but I doubt she's changed much this week." Toby was not really interested in babies. He had to text his bets for the day's football games before they started at noon. He pulled out his phone and sat at the kitchen table with his cup of coffee. "I just need to text Brian for a minute."

"Oh, man," said Adam. "I didn't even think about the games. Me too." They used the same bookie. He was unloading the bag. "What's this?" He held up the gold anklet.

"To put around her ankle," said Toby. "Tamar said it has to be on her before the whole thing even begins. Hey, are you wearing the cornicello that Mom gave us? Tamar said we all had to have those on, too. They were blessed by that holy guy in the Negev." Toby absentmindedly held out the horn-shaped pendant he was wearing.

"Oh, yeah," said Adam. "Hold on. I'll go put mine on and get this on the baby. Remind me to text Brian my picks."

"Sure thing."

"BUT THAT DOESN'T MATCH her outfit!" said Nan.

"C'mon, just indulge me," said Adam as he fastened the tiny chain around Baby Rachel's right ankle. "It's a gift from her godfather, Uncle Toby. See, she likes it." There was no noticeable difference in the baby's expression as she nursed, but Nan accepted his rationale.

Adam and Nan had only invited a few of their close friends. Half of them were not even Jewish. Adam saw it as a chance to drink and watch football with friends afterward, a welcome respite to the week of the baby shrieking and crying all night and a wife who looked nothing like the girl he'd married just eighteen months ago. His parents were at a conference in Japan that had been planned for years. His mother and father were thrilled with the birth of their fourth grandchild, but the event was not as earth-shattering as when Tamar had given birth to their first grandchild years earlier. Nan's parents weren't Jewish, so the fact that this wasn't a baptism meant that it did not even register as something important enough to fly in from Seattle.

So, when the doorbell rang half an hour later, Toby said, "Wow, someone's early. I'll get it."

Toby opened the front door to an older woman who looked like a gypsy. She was wearing a long skirt, a peasant blouse, and a colorful scarf covering her head and her cascading curly black hair. She had black kohl-lined eyes and deep burgundy lips. Her fingers were covered with silver rings, and her bracelets tinkled as she moved her arm. Toby did not recognize her.

"Hi," he said. "Come on in. You're fairly early. The rabbi's not even here yet." Tamar's flight from New York had landed late the night before, but she was not at the house yet. Toby stuck out his right hand to the woman. "I'm Toby, Adam's brother. I don't think we've met."

The gypsy looked Toby up and down. "Yes, we met a very long time ago," said the woman in heavily-accented English. "I am Batsheva, your cousin from Lithuania. I am living in Boston presently for the next few years, but I am in St. Louis for this day only."

"Oh," said Toby. "Well, it's great to meet you!"

Adam entered the room and approached Batsheva with an outstretched hand. He assumed she was a friend of Nan's. Nan had a lot of bohemian friends from art school who were interesting-looking. "Hi, I'm Adam."

"Yes," said Batsheva. "I am Batsheva."

"Adam," said Toby. "Batsheva's our cousin."

Adam scrunched his brow. "How close of a cousin are you? I know you're not a first cousin because neither of our parents has siblings."

"I am a cousin of your mother – second cousin," said Batsheva. "I have only met her twice in my lifetime."

The doorbell rang. The baby started crying. Adam nodded and turned away from Batsheva to answer the door. Fifteen other people who were friends of both Adam and Nan arrived over the next twenty minutes. Tamar was the last to arrive.

"Tamar!" Adam said. "I don't know what you need or what I'm supposed to do." She followed him into the master bedroom, where Nan was still nursing the baby.

"Hi, Nan!" said Tamar.

"Hi, Tamar," said Nan. "She's almost done. Can we start soon? Is everyone here?"

Adam nodded, then to Tamar, "Do you know our cousin, Batsheva?"

"Sounds familiar?" said Tamar vaguely. She always looked like she was only half-present in any conversation. She still had her messenger bag looped over her shoulder. She looked over at Rachel. "Oh, good. She's wearing the anklet. Do you have the other herbs and spices?" Adam nodded. Tamar took out a blue velvet bag inscribed with a symbol that Adam had never seen before. "Please put them in this bag."

Adam grabbed the bag from her. "I need to find Toby." When he found Toby, he asked, "Did you offer everyone beer and mimosas?" Toby nodded. "Good. Thanks. Hey, I need all that stuff you bought. Tamar wants it in this bag."

"Sure thing," said Toby. "I'll do it while you bring the baby out."

As soon as Baby Rachel made her appearance in the living room, all conversation died out. People smiled at the chubby baby. Nan had her wrapped in a pink blanket and handed her over to Adam. They both stood next to Tamar at a card table they had covered with a white linen tablecloth. Toby had handed out printed programs. Tamar began the prayers. When she started to bless the baby, Batsheva stood up and started walking towards the three standing adults. Tamar continued. Batsheva, who hadn't yet met Tamar, stepped next to Nan and started speaking in Hebrew. Tamar looked very surprised but nodded. Everyone else listened closely, some tried to find the Hebrew in the program, and the baby grew very quiet as if it was not breathing. Batsheva prayed and then took a large needle from within her pocket, unwrapped it, lit a lighter and waved the needle through the flame.

"What is this part?" Nan hissed at Adam.

"I don't know," he answered. "Tamar?"

"And now, our cousin, Batsheva, a blessed woman in her country and the Jewish community, must prick little Rachel's heel to allow for the elemental spirit to exit before I say the final blessing."

"No," said Nan. "No one is stabbing my daughter. I've never heard anything about this."

"I must," said Batsheva. "One drop of blood is all that the protection blessing requires. Without it, though, she may become possessed of an evil demon."

"What?!?" exclaimed Adam.

"Yes," said Tamar. "She's a scholar of the Kabbalah. Every female in our family line must do this at their baby naming. The last female who didn't was Great-great-great-great-great-aunt Esther Schmlosky. She lived many years, but as was usually the case, the demon possessed her fully at puberty. It drove out any essence of Esther. She married at the age of fifteen, as was the norm in her Polish village, but at the age of twenty, she killed her husband, her three children, and seven of her neighbors."

Adam looked at Nan. "That doesn't sound good, does it, honey?"

Nan scowled at him.

"Our family has the genetic code of Cain," said Batsheva. "The men all shed blood when their foreskins are cut for their bris. The babies are most vulnerable in the week between birth and this time. The ceremony alerts the demon who is always waiting for a body to fully inhabit. Every female in our family must spill a drop of blood at the naming to commit to their covenant with God and to expel any demon that may have already tried to attach to her soul, taken residence in the baby's body."

"No!" said Nan. "No. I won't allow this. I don't want you here. I don't know you. Get out. Go! Go!" Nan was almost hysterical. The baby started crying when she shouted.

Adam hurriedly put his hand on Batsheva's back and ushered her out of the room.

"I will leave," she said. "Tamar knows all of the special blessings for the baby. But, please, please, offer the drop of blood. I beg you." She pressed a piece of paper in Adam's hand. "Here is my phone number, my email. Contact me if you have any worries. I shall see you if you have another girl."

Before he could respond, she was out the front door.

THE BABY NAMING WAS a beautiful event except for Nan's distraught outburst. Tamar made the ceremony short, so everyone could get to beer and football. Nan excused herself to the bedroom to nurse Rachel. When Adam checked on them half an hour later, they were both asleep. He apologized to everyone that they had been up all night, and they probably wouldn't be seeing Rachel and Nan again that afternoon. The women nodded, and the men looked psyched to have unfettered football time. Adam's friend, Greg, had brought a five-foot-long submarine sandwich. Every couple had also brought brownies, chips, or potato salad. There would be plenty of leftovers, so Adam and Nan would not have to cook for a few days.

A little after six, Adam announced that everyone needed to leave and watch the evening football game on their own. They all groaned. A couple people had to be roused from napping on the sofa.

"Tamar, Toby, I couldn't have done this without you guys," Adam said as he stood at the door pressing leftover cake into their hands. "Are you sure you don't need me to take you to the airport, Tamar?"

"No, no, Toby's giving me a ride," she said. "Adam, you're going to be a great dad! I hope Nan wasn't too upset by our cousin."

"No, she's exhausted and hormonal," said Adam.

"I know how that is!" said Tamar. "Call me if you ever need any baby advice! I love you!"

They all hugged goodbye. Adam leaned against the door after they left and exhaled deeply. He had to act more enthusiastic than he really felt about these religious ceremonies, so Nan would get on board with them. He was glad the whole thing was over. He walked to their bedroom and slowly, quietly, opened the door. The baby was asleep in a bassinet against the far wall, but Nan was reading a book with a dim bedside lamp. "They've all left," he said.

"Thank God!" said Nan. "I'm so hungry!"

Adam was relieved that her mood had completely changed. They went into the kitchen. Nan gasped as she looked into the refrigerator. "It's full! Of fun food! This is wonderful!" The baby slept for two hours in a row as Nan and Adam feasted on party leftovers – three-meat sub, Italian salad, an appetizer platter with feta cheese, hummus, babaganoush, triangles of pita bread, cucumber rounds, tomatoes and banana peppers from their favorite Greek restaurant, and two different coffee cakes. "I love our friends! I had no idea all this food was here. I was so stressed with your weirdo cousin and the ceremony. I've never even been to a Jewish baby naming."

"I know, honey," said Adam. "Everyone was a little surprised when you disappeared, but they understood when I told them how little sleep you'd had. By the way, I had nothing to do with the Lithuanian cousin thing; I had no idea that she was showing up." Nan nodded with a full mouth. They made heaping plates of food and carried them into the living room where they sank into their regular spots on their lumpy but comfy couch and stretched their legs out to the coffee table.

"This is the life," sighed Nan.

"Yeah," said Adam. "The life we had two weeks ago."

Almost as if a miracle, the baby didn't start crying until the credits rolled on the movie they watched. Nan rose to feed her, and Adam cleared the plates and cups.

"Thank you, baby," Nan said to Rachel as she changed her diaper. She could have sworn that Rachel winked at her in reply.

THE NEXT AFTERNOON, Adam's secretary called Toby. "Sorry, Toby, but you're listed as Adam's emergency contact."

"What's wrong?" asked Toby

"Adam didn't come in this morning, and I can't reach him at home or on his cell," said Maxine the secretary. "He has never disappeared in the nine years that he's been at the firm. He missed two client meetings and an important strategy lunch. He has a hearing tomorrow morning, and Tim, the other attorney on the matter, is freaking out."

"Shall I go by his house?" asked Toby. "Yes, of course, I'll go by his house. It's not far."

"Thanks, Toby," said Maxine. "We're all starting to worry. Adam is never out of touch. In fact, I wouldn't mind if he didn't send me work emails on weekends..."

TWENTY MINUTES LATER, after a drive in which Toby kept repeating to his cell phone, "Call Adam," with no response, Toby reached under the flower pot on Adam and Nan's front porch for the spare key. The second he opened the door, he could smell something chemical – gas or carbon monoxide – he didn't know which. The baby was screaming. Toby left the door wide open and ran to the master bedroom as he shouted Adam's name. Adam and Nan were lying flat on their backs in bed with their eyes open wide and their mouths each open in a rictus of a horrified scream. Rachel was howling in her bassinet. The smell of her poopy diaper was worse than the gas in the air, but Toby grabbed her from the bassinet and ran out of the house. He dialed 911 as soon as he was outside. As he stood with the baby, who had stopped crying out of surprise, he thought, he noticed her clenched fist. She was clutching the broken golden chain from her ankle as she looked straight into her Uncle Toby's eyes and smiled.

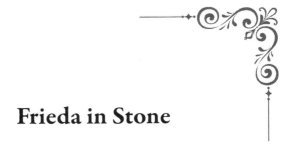

Frieda in Stone

Ken Goldman

"EXCELLENT ... ABSOLUTELY excellent ..."

Bernhard Krunstadt had created his masterpiece. This time he was certain of it. The white marble sculpture of Frieda Goldstein would be his testament, and more important than that, his salvation. He had only a bit more to do around the neck, some fine chiseling to achieve the unique feminine delicacy that had been Frieda's; afterward, he would not need to sculpt one additional chip from a new stone to attain his immortality.

Inside his studio, Krunstadt had created the sculpture entirely from memory of the woman, no mean feat for even the most talented artist. He had managed to salvage a faded old photograph of her taken at the peak of her beauty, and the likeness provided inspiration enough to turn a block of marble into a work of genius.

Of course, it would have been impossible to perfectly capture the flesh and blood Frieda in stone. It seemed miraculous that even God had created such a woman. Not so miraculous was the ease it took for one man to destroy her, and Krunstadt had spent a lifetime doing penance with his hammer and chisel.

He had traveled miles from his homeland to achieve his atonement, making a new life for himself in America to start fresh, and today it seemed his retribution would finally be paid in total. It had taken him almost fifty years to attempt capturing Frieda's likeness in stone, although his nearly completed work was more a testament to the woman's ageless beauty than to his sculpting skills.

[Yes ... she's magnificent.]

A glass of wine would go nicely now, just before he completed the finishing touches. A few sips, and when he was done with his creation, he might do justice to the rest of the bottle of Rheingau as a personal celebration of his triumph. He poured himself a small amount of the white wine, holding it to the light and studying the clear liquid inside the glass as if some lost image might appear in its luster.

["How easy it is to say you love me, Bernhard ... so easy to say the words ..."]

Krunstadt raised his glass to the woman in marble, his homage to the young nurse plucked from her hospital duties by the invading army during one night in a besieged Warsaw ghetto a thousand lifetimes ago.

"To you, Frieda, and to the brief happiness, we were never meant to share."

He drank the wine in rapid gulps, and its potent bitterness caused his head to spin so suddenly, he had to sit. Bernhard closed his eyes and remembered when the world was different, when life itself was unlike any other time.

And he remembered the girl...

...THE DARK-HAIRED GIRL with the spicy temperament who secretly shared the bed of a handsome young officer. On a winter's night, their last, while her eyes spilled with angry tears, love and hate had somehow combusted between the two to create something indefinable. A raging fire does not extinguish itself, and on that night, Bernhard could not allow its flames to consume the both of them.

"Frieda ... Frieda ... You ask too much of me."

"Too much, Bernhard? Too much? I have witnessed the Pogrom beatings and rapes in our streets. You are a powerful officer in the Wehrmacht. You know of the executions and disease here. It is not too much to ask that those in your charge allow my family to leave Warsaw and remain unharmed! My mother and father gather the remnants of their belongings, even as we speak. There is talk of refuge in Hungary for the displaced families. You have the authority to find them safe passage, Bernhard. You say you love me, but you show no love outside of this bed. Are you like the others, as much a man of stone as the figures you sculpt?"

Perhaps she truly hated him, and what passed for passion was only a despicable means to an end. He had considered this, of course. She had been given no choice when he selected her to come to his bed, and she was a shrewd enough woman to turn her circumstance to her family's advantage. Now her dark eyes locked with his, and the soothing words that should have come easily stuck inside his throat.

"Frieda, you cannot possibly understand the complexities of—"

He stopped himself. How could the woman comprehend the duty he had to his country? She was a Jewess, too arrogantly proud to recognize that destiny belonged to him and to his race. Krunstadt found the quality of her defiance oddly exciting because he admired her strength, but that same defiance also made him despise her. It was as if some odious poison grew within his heart whenever he held Frieda in his arms, and he did not know whether to make love to her all night or beat her senseless. He could never allow anyone in a position of authority to discover she shared his bed. There were none among the Geheime Staatspolizei, the Gestapo, who would have permitted Krunstadt the luxury of loving her.

"There is talk of the camps, that Warsaw is but a holding place for all of us until—"

"Enough!" he interrupted. "You ask too much! There are things which should not - and can not - be changed. Your family will be fine."

"Like all the others who are taken to Umschlagplatz?"

"Yes. Fine. All of them."

That was not exactly the truth. Umschlagplatz was the plaza to which the Warsaw Jews were regularly herded for deportation to Dachau, Buchenwald, and Sachsenhausen.

The camps.

He expected the girl was too smart to believe him even if she so desperately wanted to, and when he reached for her, Bernhard felt certain she would spit in his face. Instead, she turned away while saying nothing, and this was much worse. Krunstadt could deal with her anger more easily than her withdrawal. In later years the officer often asked himself if the girl's refusal of him that night had determined his decision.

Frieda left Officer Krunstadt's bed, insisting on joining her aged parents during this most treacherous of nights. She put on the crisp nurse's uniform whose armband displayed the six-pointed star prominently exhibiting in bold letters the word JUDE. The uniform had kept her safe until now, for medical persons were a valuable commodity among the higher-ranking officials, and none questioned the woman's frequent visits to officers of the S.S. Still, the star let no one forget what she was.

Bernhard did not stop her from leaving. It would have been foolish to try.

After midnight Krunstadt smoked the first of many cigarettes, taking the short walk to a poorly lit cross street near his quarters. From a distance, he watched as soldiers pulled Isaac and Anna Goldstein from their home. The old woman was screaming, but her husband remained silent and did not resist. Under the Warsaw moon, Frieda's elderly parents were herded at gunpoint, along with many others, into the crowded streets.

He saw Frieda push her way into the crowd, toward the soldiers standing closest to her mother. The girl was no longer wearing her nurse's uniform but instead the drab gray clothing of a factory worker worn by practically every Jew in Warsaw. Had she worn the nurse's dress, a soldier would have spotted her, would have pulled her away from the herded rabble. But this the girl clearly did not want.

"You do not have to do this, Frieda," Bernhard muttered to himself. "There is no need, no point ..."

Amid cries and shouts, Krunstadt stood too far off to hear the young woman's protests to the tall soldier holding the rifle. Her wild gesticulations suggested first pleading and then anger directed at the man who poked the weapon repeatedly into her mother's back.

Krunstadt's mind supplied the words he knew Frieda must have spoken.

"No! Don't take them, please! No! No!"

And then ...

"Damn you! Damn all of you!"

Krunstadt saw her pound the man's shoulder, watched him push her aside, and set his rifle's aim on her. Anna Goldstein noticed and threw herself between her daughter and the man, pulling at the officer's arm with such determination he almost dropped his weapon. He struck her shoulder with the butt of his rifle, and the old woman toppled near the curb. The tall soldier turned and waited for her to stagger to her feet, then shot the old woman in the head.

Hearing the crack of the gun, Isaac Goldstein looked behind for only a moment, then pulled his daughter from the tumult. Perhaps he did not recognize the supine body of his wife that lay twisted in the street, her drab clothing freckled with blood; perhaps he did not see the others step around her as if only a fallen bird lay on the ground. From afar, the old man's expression remained unreadable, and his only reaction was to quicken his pace, tugging Frieda's arm to remove her from danger.

Because the girl was not wearing her medical clothing, she would also be shot had she attempted to leave the filing mass of people. Bernhard Krunstadt thought of running to Frieda's side, revealing that this young woman was his personal nurse, that she had a permit to remain behind. But he did not move.

The girl's mother was dead, and Krunstadt knew Frieda would never abandon her father even knowing the mass of ragged workers, both young and old, was being led to the trains at Umschlagplatz. There seemed no point to rescue one who chose not to be rescued. He watched father and daughter become swallowed by the moving herd.

Bernhard remained in the streets, the crowds still shambling past him while his cigarette burned to ash. Occasionally the flash of gunfire stabbed the darkness like a sudden crack of lightning. The night had turned especially cold, and the officer tightened his collar against the harsh wind. He waited until two soldiers carried off the remains of the old woman. By then, the chill had become bitter, and Krunstadt badly wanted to return to his quarters. But there remained something he had to do.

The door to the Goldstein home had been kicked open. Krunstadt climbed the staircase to the second story and located the girl's room. As he had imagined, it was a dismal place whose plaster ceiling was badly damaged and whose gray paint was peeling everywhere. He rifled through several drawers. There was no money, of course, nothing of any value, but Krunstadt looked for only one thing.

Inside the parents' room, he found it. The photograph of Frieda must have been taken on a warm summer's day, and there in an open field, she was smiling more radiantly than Bernhard had ever seen. He quickly shoved the portrait into his pocket.

This was the woman he wished to remember. Her astonishing smile had already been significantly altered in the ghetto of Warsaw, a smile soon to be recast into something horrible. He did not want to think about the human skeleton she would become at Buchenwald, nor imagine what living atrocity into which she would have been transformed when death finally took her.

He never was given that choice. As years passed, during the darkest hours of the night, Bernhard Krunstadt lay awake imagining the girl's final days in the camp, imagining her haunted eyes hollowed like black sockets and wondering if Frieda Goldstein's last words had been screams.

THE SCULPTOR HELD THE faded photograph in his palm, losing himself in it.

Of course, the name no longer was Krunstadt, not since he had left Germany almost fifty years past, but Bernhard could never think of his identity as anything else. He cared little if the title associated with his art bore the ridiculous American name of Edgar Kornman. He knew who he was.

The '79 Rheingau had proven more effective than he had anticipated. Curiously delicious, it had diverted him from his purpose. He placed the photograph alongside the wine glass and took hammer and chisel in hand.

The girl's likeness in white marble had astounded its creator. His heart raced just looking at her reborn smile, recaptured from a moment of happiness somehow miraculously plucked from the past. Krunstadt had no idea his hands possessed such ability. But there remained the neck of his sculpture to complete, and one misguided tap of the hammer could easily annihilate his finished work. He held his chisel before him to steady his hand, then began.

"Tonight, Frieda, the burden is lifted. Tonight you release me."

He stopped himself before his hammer struck the chisel. Something was different, something not quite right. The change in the sculpture was not readily apparent, and at first, Krunstadt believed it a trick of his vision. The figure had altered only slightly, and he could not put his finger on the peculiarity. Bernhard studied his work closely before he saw.

The woman's cheekbones had hollowed somewhat, turning her face gaunt. The arms and legs also had lost muscle tone and seemed rawboned. The marble's luster had dissipated, and the stone grayed, giving the woman's likeness a wan and sickly appearance. The smile now was uncertain and tentative.

Krunstadt stepped away from his work as if from some diseased thing.

This was not the Frieda Goldstein he had sculpted!

Rationality quickly returned. The wine had been especially potent, and he had consumed an entire glass of the Rheingau rather quickly. Good wine often played nasty tricks. That had to be it. It was the wine!

But when he turned again to Frieda's marble likeness, she had grown thinner still! Her eyes had vanished inside twin darkened pits, and her body approached emaciation.

Krunstadt's lips formed a scream, but he could not make a sound, nor could he move one inch, his legs encased in concrete.

" ...and are you as much a man of stone as the figures you sculpt?" she had asked.

"Frieda, you ask too much!"

Like some filth-ridden infection, the disease had spread. The woman's chiseled smile now was gone completely, and with a movement almost imperceptible, her thin finger pointed toward the sculptor in accusation. Bernhard's mouth opened, but he could do nothing more than listen to the shrieking inside his head.

"No, Bernhard...You are the one who has asked too much!"

The gray stone of the figure crunched with movement, and the bony arms reached out to him, the sculpture a monolith of human scale struggling to be born. He could not move, could not even turn away so as not to see.

Krunstadt needed no further explanation for what seemed so unthinkable. He had not sculpted this grotesque creature he saw before him. But the lesson came a little late. The marble figure fell upon him, her bony fingers pulling him to her. Skeletal arms wrapped around him, crushing him in a lover's embrace that suggested anything but passion. He felt his bones turn brittle like dried twigs as his marble creation drew him closer while wrenching his breath from him and sapping the last remnant of his strength. Trying to push her, he caught a brief glimpse of his own hand, saw his fingers mutate before his eyes, withering as if with sudden advancing age and turning matchstick thin. He wanted to scream, wanted to howl so the whole world might hear, but his lungs retained only enough wind for him to hack and wheeze.

Frieda Goldstein pulled Bernhard closer while every bone inside him splintered, then snapped...

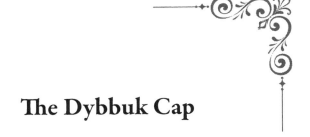

The Dybbuk Cap

Eliza Master

HADASSAH BENDS HER leg to clip on her stockings. If only she had a store-bought dress, but those were too expensive. She puts on the frock her mother has sown for her. Each handstitched seam is perfectly straight. It is a pretty coral color but tight around her breasts, almost too small. Hadassah sighs loudly.

"Hyman is a gute boy," says Hadassah's mother in response. She is standing on the other side of the curtain that serves as a door for the closet bedroom. The real bedroom is occupied by her five brothers.

"But I'm not tired," Joseph screeches from the bedroom.

"If you don't get in bed, a Dybbuk ghost will come take your place. They love to sleep in the empty beds of naughty children," warns her mother from the other room.

Her parents sleep in the pantry among the bags of flour and dusty jars of pickles. There they made her youngest brother, Joseph. He is two and needs constant attention. Hadassah secretly plans to never have children.

Her thoughts return to Hyman. He brought the family a brisket last Sabbath as a gift from his father, the butcher. It had been months since the family of eight had eaten meat. Sometimes they ate chicken, but mostly bread and beans. It is no wonder the whole family wants Hadassah to marry Hyman.

"I'll help you," her mother shoots the curtain back. She frowns while pinching Hadassah's cheeks to make them rosy. There is a knock on the apartment door.

"Good evening, Mr. Gevins," says Hyman to her father.

Hadassah steps out, ready to go. Her father is wearing his shabby flat cap, covering his unwashed hair.

Joseph runs out in pajamas despite Bubbe's dybbuk tale. He grabs her hand saying, "Take me with you." But she brushes him off and turns to her guest.

"Hi Hymie," she says kindly. She remembers how he cried after Hebrew school when the bigger boys tugged his red side locks. But he looks different at sixteen, with a downy beard. His biceps bulge from hefting carcasses in the shop.

"Hello, Hada," says Hyman shyly.

Her mother nudges her, and she moves next to him. Hyman grasps her hand, but her father's gaze follows the motion. He lets go.

"We're going to the rides at Penn's landing. I'll bring her back by 9:30," Hyman talks too loudly, making Hadassah feel chilled. A wind blows up her spine, and she coughs.

They sit side by side on the streetcar without exchanging a word. Everyone else is quiet too. Outside Philadelphia bustles with horses and foot traffic.

As they step off, Hyman says, "hot dogs." Once again, he grabs Hadassah's hand. This time he pulls her. They go straight to Nathan's. The kosher hot dogs are smothered in relish and come in a fat bun. Hadassah devourers hers. It is delicious.

Hyman buys tickets to the Ferris wheel, and they get into a chair. Even though the wheel moves slowly, Hadassah is frightened to be so far above the ground. Right after they come to the peak, the Ferris wheel freezes. Far below, Hadassah sees a family get into an empty chair. She straightens her back and prays for the ride to start again.

In one motion, Hyman puts his arm around Hadassah and gives her a sloppy kiss. She pulls away, pressing herself into the chair cushion. Hyman wears a confident grin.

Hadassah waits until the wheel starts again and says, "Take me home."

That night she lays awake on her bed with the curtain closed. She scratches the inside of her wrist until it is raw, drawing out uninvited tears. The scratch has turned into a red line. Fortunately, her school blouse will hide it.

Tomorrow Hadassah will be back at the Philadelphia Girls' Normal School. There she fills her mind with mathematics and science. She has been promoted two grades and will graduate as valedictorian, even though she is only fifteen.

PRINCIPAL SHUSTER ASKS Hadassah to participate in community service. She wants to tutor at Durham Negro School because she knows they don't teach past sixth grade. The principal sends a letter to arrange her visit.

At breakfast, Hadassah says, "I'm going to be studying after school." She lies to her parents about volunteering at Durham school. She takes a nickel from her brother's tin bank for the streetcar.

That afternoon, Hadassah rides four stops to Durham school. The last one has an overturned garbage can. She is the only white left on the trolley. A rodent scurries away as she steps to the curb. This is her first time in West Philadelphia.

The auditorium is overflowing with young people. She imagined the class would only be a handful of kids at desks. She has never spoken in front of an audience.

Hadassah hunches behind the podium. The room quiets, waiting for her.

Bravely she begins, "Hello, students, I am Hadassah Gevins, and I want to be a teacher." Everyone applauds. There is a girl in the front row with wide cheeks and friendly eyes. It is calming to pretend she is the only one listening. Sitting next to her is the most beautiful man Hadassah has ever seen. The class goes better than expected.

Afterward, the girl with the friendly eyes comes up. "Thank you very much,'" she says politely. "I'm Althea, and I want to be a teacher too." She invites Hadassah to visit on Sunday.

HADASSAH DOESN'T ASK for permission to visit Althea. Instead, she tells her parents she is going by the butcher shop to meet Hyman.

Althea lives on the third floor of a boarding house a few blocks from Durham School. Hadassah scoots around a lady smoking a cigarette on the marble stoop. A stair splits under her foot as she walks upstairs. Softly, she knocks on the door marked, O. Jones.

"This is my mother, Octavia," says Althea, smiling graciously.

"Very nice to meet you," says Octavia, reaching down to shake Hadassah's hand. Althea's mother is tall with a warm voice.

Tentatively, Hadassah glances around. The whole place is just one room with a large sink and a coal brazier for cooking. Metal dishes are stacked neatly, and she sees folded sleeping pallets on the floor. An open window lets in a small breeze. Everything is clean, and there is a lemony scent.

Althea and Hadassah sit at a small table with two chairs. Octavia goes to buy some eggs. The girls are going over multiplication tables when a black cat wanders in from the fire escape. It meows to Althea.

"Hi, Blacky," Althea coos. She fills a cup with milk and gives it to the cat.

Hadassah was taught never to waste food on an animal. But this one is clean with shiny fur. Blacky brushes against her leg, and she pets his back with her fingertips. After the milk is gone, Blacky curls up on Althea's lap for a nap.

The door bursts open. Blacky jumps off and runs out the open window to a metal fire escape. The beautiful man from the auditorium enters. He is wearing a poplin flat cap and tan slacks.

"My brother Vincent," says Althea, smiling. Hadassah coughs awkwardly but manages to introduce herself. She thinks the Jones must be the most handsome family in all of Philadelphia.

Vincent follows the cat outside and sits on the fire escape polishing a trumpet. From her seat, Hadassah watches as he takes off his flat cap and stuffs it into the trumpet horn. He blows a few experimental blows and adjusts the cap until he is satisfied with the sound. The fire escape creaks as he bounds upwards and out of view.

Hadassah is concentrating on the textbook when she hears the trumpet. She has never heard this kind of music, but she knows it is called jazz. Both women take a moment to listen. The music is mournful and sweet. It makes Hadassah want to dance.

ON MONDAY, HADASSAH has a coughing fit at school. She collapses in the cafeteria. Everyone backs away, fearing contagion. After she recovers, the janitor walks her home. Hadassah gets worse with a fever. She coughs up blood. The doctor comes and prescribes bed rest and quarantine. Joseph, her baby brother, sneaks into the bed with her and falls asleep. Hadassah doesn't awaken when her mother yanks him out.

Hadassah misses her next class at Durham. Althea gets her address from the high school. She brings Vincent to the apartment. Hadassah's mother opens the door.

"Hello, Mrs. Gevins," says Althea. "We are Hadassah's students from Durham School." Vincent removes his cap respectfully and holds it in his hands.

It is Saturday, and the men are all at synagogue. Hadassah's mother is surprised that her daughter knows black people. She looks them up and down suspiciously. She decides they are harmless and opens the bedroom curtain. Vincent gazes at the pale girl in the bed.

In response, Hadassah's eyes flutter open for the first time today. Her heart beats heavily, thunking against the inside of her ribs. The thunks race like a stone crashing down a mountain. They batter the breath out of her lungs. Abruptly her heart stops.

Her spirit is limber and free. She jumps towards Vincent and lands in the flat cap he is holding. The cap smells like starch and yesterday's rain. And Vincent. She is happy.

It takes a minute to realize that she has died and become a dybbuk, like the ones from her bedtime stories. But she is still Hadassah, not a scary ghost. Happiness slinks away as loss moves in.

Hyman lets himself into the apartment. He is carrying a lamb chop that he sets on the kitchen counter. He gives Vincent and Althea a steely look, so they move aside.

Hadassah tries to yell from the flat cap that she has died, but there is no sound.

Somehow her mother hears her. She pushes her way into the alcove and listens for breath, but it is gone. She shouts, "Why, God? Why have you taken my daughter!" Then she wails and punches herself in the chest repeatedly.

Hyman begins to cry. He falls to his knees at the foot of Hadassah's bed and chants the Kaddish, "Yit'gadal v'yit'kadash sh' mei raba..."

"I want Hada!" screams Joseph, interrupting. The boy tries to run into the alcove, but Hyman blocks his way.

"She's gone now, Joseph. Only God knows where," says Hyman.

Though the cap is soft and warm, Hadassah wants to be with her family and tell them she is alive. She collects all her energy to try to move back into her body. But she is stuck. Vincent puts the cap on his head and grabs Althea's hand.

"We'll be going now," Vincent says to the room. Everyone ignores them as they step out quietly.

Hadassah journeys back to Althea's in the cap. Vincent hangs it on a hook by the door. Althea is tired and lies on her pallet even though it is afternoon. Blacky comes in and cuddles up against her back, and they let him stay. Octavia makes fresh tea, but the girl is sweating too much to drink any. They take turns wiping her forehead with a cold washcloth to bring down the fever. Even though the hospital is nearby black patients are not allowed. Anyway, there is no money for doctoring. Althea coughs up clots of blood.

Her mother misses work and loses her job as a house cleaner. "It is the white girl's fault," says Octavia to Vincent.

Hadassah knows it is true. She is the cause of Althea's sickness. Why did she ever go to Durham school and infect these good people?

Vincent spends most of his time on the roof, playing sad tunes on the trumpet. He wears the flat cap all the time because he feels shivery and cold. Hadassah shivers along with him and worries.

In two days, Althea is dead. Vincent wraps her body in an old tablecloth and brings her to the Strangers' Ground, an open grave behind the Baptist church.

Two weeks later, he brings his mother there, also dead from the consumption. Hadassah goes with him in the cap. She hasn't seen the ghosts of Althea or her mother. Are dybbuks only from dead Jews, she wonders? Or is she the only ghost in Philadelphia?

VINCENT IS BEHIND ON the rent, so he takes a job load-
ing coal for the Pennsylvania Railroad. His lungs hurt from the
dust, and his throat is sore.

"Here, take this." Hadassah watches a coworker pull his
bandana off and hand it to Vincent. He says, "So you don't
breathe in the dust."

After work, they find a secluded spot on the Schuylkill River and strip for a swim. Hadassah watches from the cap as they
frolic in the water. The friend jumps on Vincent's shoulders and
tries to push his head under playfully. Then they are entwined.
Hadassah sees the muscles flex in Vincent's back. They move in
slow jerks for a few minutes before separating and swimming
back to shore.

Vincent puts the cap on while he is stark naked. The guys
both laugh out loud. Then they hear footsteps, so they dress
quickly and sneak away. Over the next week, Vincent swims
with his new friend every day. At night he picks up the trumpet
and stuffs the cap in as a mute. The buoyant tones reverberate
through Hadassah's dybbuk soul. She imagines she is the one
swimming with Vincent.

The humid Philadelphia summer arrives, and Vincent
leaves his cap in the trumpet all day while he is at work. Hadassah sleeps while he is gone. Blacky wanders to the window and
mews, but there is no one to let him in.

On a dusky morning, she is awoken abruptly as Vincent
yanks the cap out of the trumpet horn and shakes it out. He
places it on his head, pressing out each panel with his fingers in
front of a mirror. Hadassah notices small wrinkles have sprout-

ed from the corners of his eyes. Suddenly, Vincent shouts at himself, "Ellis!" His cheeks are wet with tears.

Vincent and Hadassah leave the apartment and march the ten blocks to the train station. They wait on the platform by the tracks. A train pulls in with a searing screech.

"Ellis," whispers Vincent softly as his friend approaches. Ellis' gaze pounds like a hammer. The men shake hands stiffly. Then Ellis boards the train without looking back.

Vincent drags his feet home. It's hot, so he opens the window and Blacky comes in. He undresses, leaving his flat cap on the floor. Then he gets in bed and faces the wall. Blacky slinks over to Hadassah's cap and plunks down.

"Meow," he says to Hadassah. The animal can sense her. She allows herself to get lost in the scent of his luxurious fur. It has been too long since anyone has been aware of her. She drinks in all she can.

There is a loud knocking on the door. Vincent stands up and answers, wearing only boxers.

"Excuse me. Are you the cat who plays the horn?" says a neatly dressed man. He is wearing a blue suit with a thin black tie.

"Yes, that'd be me," replies Vincent.

"Horn sounds real nice," says the man continuing. "Today is Election Day. And me and some friends were hoping to get a new man for president, Mr. Roosevelt. The voting machine is right there in Durham school. I could walk you there if you want to vote."

Vincent dresses, leaving the cap behind. It turns to dark night. Hadassah falls asleep. Firecrackers blast echoing against the buildings. Blacky darts out the window. The door bursts open, and Vincent grabs his trumpet. He puts the cap on and races back outside.

The street is clear of horses and wagons and flooded with people. Hadassah sees that there is a pile of wood on the corner. Fence boards, broken chairs, and an old spinning wheel are stacked for the voting day bonfire. A trail of youth arrives with more scraps to burn.

Then a tall boy brings a jerrycan of gasoline. He drenches the pile and throws on a lit match. Flames shoot up, glimmering off the row houses. The brick walls look like they are made of gold.

As if on cue, the men pull off their caps and toss them in the air. Vincent tosses Hadassah high above the other caps. She can see the top of the bonfire. The flames flicker and dance. Then she falls in.

As each fiber of the cap burns, Hadassah feels lighter. She rises up, leaving the ash behind. Beneath her is Vincent. He is laughing as he brings the trumpet to his lips.

Hadassah rides the notes high above the Philadelphia night until the earth looks like a marble.

Fat Fidl

Marc Morgenstern

THE TALMUD SAYS A MIRACLE doesn't happen every day. Sixty-three books containing the wisdom of the ages, but I, Mikha Grinblat, say the Talmud is wrong in this case. On any one particular day—sunny or cloudy, but especially cloudy—a miracle can occur. On that day, water may not be made into wine, but with an apple or two, it can become vinegar good enough for pickling.

I was leaving today for New York City: the new world, which I pictured as a bejeweled place, sitting high on a hill surrounded by smooth, silver water. A place for miracles. In other words, everything that our shtetl was not. Kasrilevka huddled close to the ground, dirt poor and Jewish—really the same thing. You'd think we would be left alone in our simmering little pot; what was there to plunder? Who was there to worry about—my father, Isaak the grinder? My mother, Rivka the pickler? Me? Still, the pogroms drew closer every day—mobs convinced that we, meager Jews, threatened their great empire.

My valise, overstuffed and strangled with rope to keep everything in, sat by the door. Next to it stood my fidl case, wide-hipped and thin-necked like a lady. They would be my only companions on the journey: days by train, then the ship from Hamburg, weeks more at sea. I'd never been farther from home than Minsk. In Kasrilevka, I knew everyone—sometimes too well. Soon, with hundreds of strangers, I would be all by myself.

Father approached me with head bowed and eyes closed, lips moving in prayer. Still, he managed to find my hand and place into it a small object, the size and heft of two stones. Rolled over and over in last week's newspaper, tied with string and sealed with blood-red wax, it looked like a wounded fist.

"Until you get to America, do not open it," he said. "Absolutely don't, or I cannot vouch for what may happen to you. You might encounter a disreputable woman. You might fall overboard. I don't know." He looked at the earthen floor and then sideways at me, his only son, with a mix of fear and love. His eyes floated in tears, not knowing when he might see me again. "A little goyisha you might become."

"There's no such thing as a little goyisha," I said. "A Jew you are or not, Father. No pilpul. Either pepper or salt. Black or white."

At my own joke, I laughed—"pilpul" meaning Talmudic debate, but also hot pepper. The hearty laugh of a young man certain he knows better than the old one. After all, I was going to America to start my true life. Soon, others in the family Grinblat would follow (that was our hope and prayer)—but when? They were counting on me—a mere nineteen-year-old musician with an infant's English vocabulary—to establish a suitable Jewish home on another continent.

Onto my shoulder, my father tenderly laid a big paw—the same one that wrapped his gift. He was the shtetl grinder, hands rasped as if he tested all his tools on them. He probably had, being a diligent man. Also, a generous one who gave customers credit. On a less generous day, he bartered for cabbage. Not a man who'd ever used a real fist. Neither was I.

Like the tailor or baker's sons, I'd been expected to take on father's trade. He'd patiently shown me how to hold the knife just so under the stone grinding wheel. Angle it properly to achieve the sharpest edge. But my hands were soft and awkward; knives would slip out and plummet to earth. One landed blade first on the toe of my boot. Fortunately, they were thick sheepskin.

One day, a traveler came through with a wooden box of cutlery, an entire family of clattering knives. Once prosperous, the man now offered not kopeks for my father's services, but a groyse fidl in trade. What, you may ask, is a groyse fidl? Picture in your mind a violin that's eaten too many potatoes, not boiled but cooked in butter. An enlarged and fattened violin with a deeper sound and three strings instead of four. I begged Father to accept it. With unscarred hands pressed fervently together, I promised to practice and learn. And I did, so that I came to perform at weddings, bar mitzvahs, simkhes and sometimes, sadly, at funerals. Songs and songs for all occasions in my head, with never a need to write them down.

On my last day in the kitchen, the fidl cowered in the instrument case as if afraid for itself and me. I wore my old boots, knife scar now erased from the toe—a parting favor from Schuster, an esteemed member of my father's minyan. The toes shined with linseed oil. I clicked the repaired wooden heels and bowed like the traveling musician I'd soon be, hat in hand.

"You must always walk like you know where you are going," Father said, "even when you don't. Especially then."

"How else would I walk?" I said with a weak grin, trying to bring some light into the kitchen.

"My son," Mother sobbed, "Mikha'el." On her lips this day, my name sounded different—like she'd just named me for the first time, like I was the only Mikha'el in the world, a world taking me far away, maybe for good. One hand beat her chest like a professional mourner while the other dangled a burlap sack full of her famous pickles. My little sister, Elena, hugged me hard, leaving a puddle on my shoulder. For herself, she wept, wanting so desperately to come along. Ever cautious, my father wouldn't allow it.

IN HAMBURG THREE DAYS later, the SS Auguste Victoria lay like a floating Minsk, portholes blinking with lanterns, belly swallowing up cargo. Smoke belched from its stacks, staining the air. The dock shook from the engines and a herd of people clucking, squawking, and stomping. Some called out to me "bompkin!"—ordering me to buy whatever they were selling: mattress, pot, apple, secret remedy for seasickness. But I knew better and also didn't want to take my hand off my own goods for one instant. With thieves' hands grabbing all around, I clutched my fidl tightly to my chest.

A shrill whistle blew, and I fell in line with others, all bearing their donkey's load.

"Oy! See them," sneered the man next to me.

"See who?" I patted the pocket bearing Father's gift to make sure it was still there.

"Them, up there. First-class." He pointed up and up through the wooden grate and towards the fading light. There they were, in fancy clothes on the top deck, last rays of the sun shining only upon them.

"Who are they? Some Rothschilds?" I said, trying to sound as carefree as he did, even more so. He told me his name was Josef, twenty-two years of age, from a city unknown to me in Germany.

"You can read, bompkin, can't you?" he said, handing me a list of names printed on thick paper. Yiddish and Hebrew, I could read. A little Russian. But English? Luckily, he couldn't stop himself. "Imagine that: Baron de Rothschild himself, the richest man in the world. And Mrs. Charles Frederick Theodore Steinway, widow of the piano maker." He pointed at the instrument case clutched under my arm. "A musician like you must know what a pianoforte is, bompkin, yes?"

"Of course I do." From my musician friends, I had heard talk of something called a grand piano: a whole orchestra, it was said, in a huge, polished wooden box. Heard talk, but neither heard nor seen one.

"Jews, just like you and me," he said. "Only rich."

Observing his age, schnoz, and hat, I had to agree that we looked indeed similar, almost like two brothers. Except that a woman hid behind him, so silent in the tumult, I'd not noticed her at first, as quiet as he was noisy. She held tightly onto his arm, looking down and not at me. Even with babushka shadowing her face, she was comely.

"This is Sheyna," he said. "She and I will marry in the United States of America."

"Mikha," I said, nodding to each in turn. "Unmatched." I blushed, wishing to have said anything else. Truth was: nineteen years of age, and I had not yet benefitted from successful yenta's work, let alone had my arm squeezed by a woman other than my mother or sister.

I followed Josef and Sheyna down narrow stairs as steep as any ladder, valise slapping my leg hard with each step. Unlike Noah of the ark, the officer at the bottom step separated the couples, waving men to the left and women to the right. Josef and Sheyna parted with bereft looks over their shoulders. They would not see each other until we were next allowed on deck and who knew when that would be. I continued two-by-two with Josef to a large chamber stacked with wooden berths for storing people like so much firewood—more people than ever lived in our village.

THE VOYAGE WENT WELL enough for a time.

Except for the double stink: next week's meals stored in barrels below and people crammed into steerage shoulder to shoulder, ass to ass, like so many pickled herring. Except for my eating through the sack of Mother's gherkins—anything to avoid the slop served from filthy cauldrons, unfit even for farm animals. I lusted for mangel-wurzel—chicken feet—what Mother would put in soup to hint at meat when we couldn't afford the genuine article. I tried the hard biscuits but stopped after Josef injured a tooth on one.

Nursing the tooth with his tongue, he talked about what we'd eat upon landing in New York City: wursts exploding with juice at first bite; fat chickens running through streets, free for the plucking. The more we talked, the hungrier I became. Pulling the last pickle out of my burlap sack, I held it under my nostrils. I'd intended to save it until beholding the giant woman welcoming us to New York City, torch held high. I'd planned to greet her with a loud and thankful crunch of my Russian pickle. The scent of dill and beloved garlic, however, stirred visions of Kasrilevka and my mother at her barrel of brine, humming the folk song I'd just played for her.

I closed my eyes and took a bite.

Unfortunately, the gherkin did not bite back; it was without crunch, mealy, and bland. Opening my eyes, I found it mold-green on the outside, bleached white on the inside. The pickle hung limply from my hand, feeling sorry for itself. At that moment, I wanted nothing more than Mother stroking my cheek and Father's hand on mine, guiding me at the grinding stone. Why had I left them? Why had they let me? My empty belly ached at the thought.

FIVE DAYS OUT AND EQUALLY far from my old home and new one, the ocean got mad. How we might have wronged the almighty I don't know, but he punished us with black churns of waves, rain without end and evil blasts of wind. For hours and days, the boat rose with his anger and plummeted back down. Each time, I banged my head on the bunk above. All around me, poor souls retched and shat into buckets overflowing, sloshing to the floor. Whimpers, whines, cries for mercy shot out of the dark.

I prayed into the emptiness: Dear God, why have you forsaken me? Punching my chest with my fist, I waited. And waited.

Rather than a thundering from clouds above, a small voice finally rose from the bunk below me. "Mikha, what have you to complain about?" Josef moaned.

"Everything," I said in the same grieving tone. "I should have studied harder at the shul. I should have worked more diligently to learn Father's trade. I should not have abandoned my mother and my sister." I tried to rend my garment, but it was too soaked to rip. "No wonder this endless storm was sent to us." The beams creaked loudly in agreement.

"That is nothing," Josef said. The ship dove again, and we rolled and thudded together against the wall. "I've not seen my beloved for days. I have no idea how she fares. If we ever get out of this alive, we will marry now—no more waiting for a country we might never see."

I crawled out of my bunk and staggered to the foot of the stairs that had brought us down to this hole. The grate at the top reflected feeble light. Beyond it, I knew a sailor stood guard, ensuring passengers in steerage stayed there during the storm. Foul liquid covered the toes of my boots. Stench filled my nostrils. Josef coughed and heaved into a bucket.

"Sailor," I yelled in German. "Let me out!"

I climbed halfway up the steep steps, holding on to the handrail for dear life as the ship lurched. "Let me out. I need air." Two more steps up, and I could just make out a blue and white striped cap and beneath it, a face—smooth and young, almost gold from his candle's glow.

"Landsmann, nein," he said, and smiled through the grate. Not an evil leer looking down upon me; no Haman's face to make it easier for me to despise him. Instead, an open farm face on a man my age, probably a bompkin like me.

"Fruend," I tried. "Bitte?"

"Nein," he said.

"Why do you lock us here? Are we not like you?"

"For your own safety," he said, without a crumb of apology.

"Hah!" was all I could think to say to this yankel. We both knew he truly meant the safety of first-class, not us lowly, suffering creatures at the bottom of the boat.

The boat tumbled on the very next wave, tossing me downstairs toward the floating murk below. I caught myself against the edge of my bunk and somehow pulled myself onto it. Pain knifed my side. Father's gift! I lifted out the package, patting my hands all over it like the blind village idiot, now finding: red sealing wax cracked, newspaper wrapping wet, and falling to pieces. Unreadable—the past washed away.

"Oy, will this never end!" Josef cried from below.

Maimonides teaches us that every man must exercise his own free will. We, he asserts, are not sheep. We alone must make our own decisions and determine our futures. I'd promised my father I would not open his gift before reaching America. But what if his package needed help?

I lit a precious candle. With a peel of paper here, a slip of twine there, I assisted my father's package in opening itself. Inside, the sharp-edged pieces of a miniature clay man: head with sleeping features and barely a neck, one four-toed foot, and one three-fingered hand. His injured extremities grasped the last folds of paper with desperation.

A golem. My father had given me a golem.

"Ach!" I cried to God, Josef, and Isaak Grinblat, hoping all would be listening. I cupped my hand to my ear to better hear their reply.

From God and Josef, I heard nothing.

The name Isaak means laughing man; I could almost hear my father—not gleeful, but huffing and snorting—furious at the state of his gift.

What's a golem, you might ask? A dumb dirt figure that, once animated by man, performs his bidding and then some. History be told, it's a miracle worker who's saved ghettos from destruction, but only for a time; a Jewish good luck charm that, like all things Jewish, is bound to turn unlucky soon. Not unlike having a Shabbat gentile who lights the home lamps, then burns down the house. My father must have thought I would need its perilous power later in America. The middle of the angry Atlantic on the Hamburg-Amerika Line, I decided, was close enough.

I whispered into one chipped clay ear: "Golem, please help me."

Perhaps it was a gust of wind entering from the lone porthole, but I felt a rustling on my own ear. Open your case and play, the Golem whispered back to me.

I stood for the first time in days and braced my shaky legs against the wooden bunks. Brown, foul water still sloshed over the tips of my boots, but I couldn't care less. At first, the groyse fidl felt like a stranger in my hands—heavy and stiff. I kissed its fat body to become reacquainted, tasting the sweet spruce.

It grabbed my chin and kissed me back. One by one, I tenderly tuned each string.

Lounging in my bunk, the Golem seemed to form a smile.

My bow drew dreck: creaky complaints of where have you been? Off-key protests of how could you have neglected me? Sharp strings bit at my fingertips. Before long, though, my fidl found its heart. It wailed for our stomachs, our bones, and families left behind. For all of the steerage, my fidl lamented, sad sound finding every corner of our hole.

And what happened then? Not a parting of the sea. Not a loud summons from the shofar. Bit by bit, however, the slap of rain let up, the wind eased its roar, and for the first time in days, the soft sound of breathing could be heard. In blessed quiet, steerage slept. Having done its work, Golem nestled in my pocket and slept, too—eyes closed, body at peace.

THE NEXT DAY ROSE LIKE Adi's first morning before he bit into the bad fruit. The sky clear, sea flat, air salty and awake, the stink swept away.

"Your music. Such a mitzvah!" exclaimed Josef, his mouth inches from my ear. He stood on his two feet for the first time in days.

"My dear father was wrong."

"Such disrespect on such a morning! Why scorn your father today of all days when you have done such a mitzvah with your fidl?" Indeed, Jews and Gentiles alike paraded by my bunk, nodding and knocking on planks in gratitude. Their knuckles must have awakened Golem because he stirred in my pocket. I pulled him out and laid him lovingly on the bunk. Josef gasped at the sight of him.

"Father gave me this as a parting gift, but with a solemn vow," I said. "I was not to open it until we reached America, or who knows what might befall me—or us." Josef jumped back as if seeing a ghost. Who could blame him? Such a sight: cracked clay man, so wounded by the voyage, yet still smiling.

"But you did open it, and the seas did calm themselves," Josef said at last. "What can be wrong with one tiny little miracle?" He stared at the Golem, then at me, and again at the Golem, but came no closer to us.

"You've heard tell of Golems," I said. "Once summoned, they never stop when you want them to."

From above came the sound of a screeching hinge, rusted and unused. The grated door at the top of the stairs smacked open against the deck. A sailor cried: "You may rise."

No rabbi's call was more dear to me. No invitation to bless the challah at the Shabbat table more welcome. I jumped out of the bunk and, with the Golem safely in my jacket pocket, led the people of steerage upstairs. Oh, the light, like the sun, was born today! The air, like the first air ever breathed by man!

On deck, Josef's face danced with the promise of seeing his beloved again. His feet paced in anticipation. After a long line of passengers, Sheyna finally stepped out, her long cow's eyelashes fluttering in the brightness. She struck me as thinner and paler than before, but still comely—even more so when she opened her heart-shaped mouth and told the story of glimpsing death's door itself. Sheyna was so excitable that in describing her fever and bodily distress, she forgot her modesty; her babushka slid to her shoulders, revealing chestnut hair and shapely collar-bone. As they embraced, my head filled with wool, my eyes blurred. I grabbed the rail to steady myself.

"Rabbi!" Josef yelled into the milling crowd. "Is there a rabbi to marry us?"

A man stepped forward wearing hat and tallit, damp and stained but still faithfully hugging his neck. A woman placed a white handkerchief as a veil atop Sheyna's head. Josef motioned for me to stand by his side. And thus they were married—without chuppah or ring, but with all of the steerage as witnesses to the blessed event.

Someone found a drinking glass and—dear as it was to us travelers—placed it under Josef's boot. With the resounding crack of his heel, I began to play.

I fiddled like never before—for my new friend and his wife, for the wife I did not have, for my parents at home. I bowed furiously and fingered masterfully, as if I were playing for all fiddlers everywhere, at every wedding that had ever been. From my pocket, the Golem's little hands clapped rhythm, driving me without company of violin, cello, or clarinet. For hours, I played alone as everyone danced circle upon circle with the bride and groom swirling in the very center, ship churning ever closer to America.

WHEN I FINALLY STOPPED playing, the sun sagged in the western sky before us. Wedding guests sat crumpled and exhausted on the deck. My bowing arm hung limp and spent from my shoulder, fingers weeping with pain. Someone handed me a rag to wipe my sweaty face and fidl, still warm to the touch.

Out of the corner of my eye, like a vision, a uniformed servant marched in my direction. He could not be coming for a fidl-playing bompkin from a village not even close to Minsk. Yet he halted in front of me, his white gloves holding out a tray. On it was a thick paper card with hand lettering: Bratschist.

"Take it, Mikha," Josef said from behind me. "It's for you, Mr. Viola Player." I took the card from the tray as instructed. "Now, bompkin, turn it over, if you please." When I hesitated, he pulled the card from my hand and read: "Please join me at the First Class Music Lounge at seven o'clock this evening. Signed, Anton Seidl."

"Whoever this Anton Seidl is, it must be a joke or worse yet, a wager at my expense," I said, scanning the first-class deck as if the man might be up there regarding us. "Why else would someone like me be summoned someplace like that?"

"You've never heard of Maestro Seidl from Budapest, now conductor of the greatest orchestra in New York City?" He peered into my confused face. "And he wants you to play for him?" The servant stood before us, mute, awaiting a response. "Please tell the Maestro that the Bratschist and his second would be honored to join him this evening," Josef instructed him. To me, he added: "And you will be honored to play. Imagine the chances!"

It struck me like the back of a hand from above: Golem. Since last night, I had not whispered again into his ear nor begged for his intervention. I'd thought he was sleeping, tired like me from our labors. This invitation must be his unbidden work, taking my life into his clay hands without even a May I? I pulled Golem out of my pocket, less lovingly this time. He emerged in two pieces: body now separated from his head.

Peering deeply into heavily-lidded eyes, I didn't know whether to thank him or beg him to leave me alone. Still, to play for a renowned Maestro...

THAT EVENING, THE SAME servant came to fetch us. I'd tossed barrel water into my armpits. Deep in my valise, I found my other shirt—no cleaner than the first but less worn. I swiped sea salt off my fidl case. For my last preparation, I slipped Golem back into my jacket pocket, asking: How many miracles in one day?

Josef and I followed the servant up and up from steerage to second class, then to first class. I'd never climbed so many stairs, nor felt so many eyes upon me, all inquiring: what are these two steerage Jews doing here? I hugged my fidl case and yanked down my shtetl cap as if it might protect me. Even with a broken Golem in my pocket, who was I fooling? Especially with a Golem in my pocket. Josef, for his part, raised his ample nose skyward and jutted out his chin as if he belonged up here.

"Calm yourself, bompkin," he said. But my heart pounded a dancing beat. My stained boots put one foot in front of another.

We entered a room with walls covered in velvet as if inside the tsar's jewel box. Tobacco smoke hung in the air, illuminated by fancy gas lamps. They gave ghostly halos to the audience before us—two men and a woman. In the middle of the room, the pianoforte floated like a wooden vessel, its open-top a harp-shaped sail. Thick strings glittered from within.

"Herr Seidl, Madame Steinway, Herr Rothschild," the servant announced. I bowed feverishly, indeed more than once to each of them.

"May I present Herr Mikha Grinblat," Josef's voice rang out. "Bratschist außergewöhnlich." At that moment, I regarded myself as anything but an "extraordinary violist"—just a groyse fidl player far away from home.

Herr Seidl, resplendent in a black suit and stiff white tie and shirt, flung back his tails and sat down at the piano bench. Anxious bow shook in my hand. I had no idea why he had summoned me to the music lounge, let alone what he might want me to play. He hit a single note—middle C. I nervously, quietly, made sure I was in tune.

"Traurig," he barked. He meant the "sad" funeral lamentation I'd played the night before. Placing bow to strings, I took a deep breath of smoky air. The mournful song began slowly and softly, then gathered itself, then flew from my instrument. Could all my friends below hear it? My fidl crying for them from first class?

The pianoforte erupted, sounding like dozens of hands playing. The Maestro took hold of my shtetl dirge and spun notes inside and around it that I had never heard before. His intricate lace knit with my rough wool, filling the night. If only my parents could have been watching, listening... A specter came into focus behind my closed eyes—Golem, suddenly the size of a man, sitting at the pianoforte, his remaining fingers pressing keys with mad love. He smiled back at me, and I thought: Golem, how could I have so misjudged you?

We played and played until the Maestro's hands halted, and applause began. I opened my eyes to see Madame Steinway, whose name was imprinted in gold on this very piano and Herr Rothschild, the richest man in the world. Each a Jew! Herr Seidl—not the Golem—sat erectly on the bench, applauding as well. It struck me that he knew the music intimately and well. A Jew was a Jew was a Jew.

"Herr Grinblat," Seidl said. "Such a young man playing with the skill and feeling of an experienced musician."

"Yes, a true artist, worthy of a chair in a fine New York City orchestra," Josef jumped in. I pictured myself in the same fine clothes Seidl now wore, nestled among a hundred similarly attired men, each with instrument shining.

"All you need is one more viola string," Madame Steinway. Everyone nodded politely.

"Thanks to you, Herr Seidl," I said meekly to him, but really to Golem, who was changing my life's course. And to my father Isaak, who'd gifted me Golem in the first place.

The Maestro reached under the elegant body of the pianoforte and brought out folded white sheets of paper inscribed with black markings.

"Well then, shall we play something else, Herr Grinblat?" he said. "How about the Bruch Concerto? Technically for the viola, but I am sure you are quite capable." He spread the music across the top of the piano like a path. All I needed to do was follow it.

Simple. But I had never learned how to read music.

THE NEXT MORNING, JOSEF, Sheyna, and I looked out from the rail at the city before us. Rather than jeweled, New York appeared grey and charred, like the inside of a thousand chimneys. As promised all those days at sea, the Statue of Lady Liberty greeted with her torch, but also her inscribed tablets with no meaning to me.

Standing there, I recall we waited without talking—even Josef was silent for once. First-class must leave the ship first, with all its trunks full of evening finery. Then second-class. Then, we in steerage would be transferred to smaller boats for the trip to Ellis Island.

With my strangled valise and fat fidl case, I waited for my new life to begin. The fractured Golem weighed in my pocket. As in all the stories, it had served—and failed— me, bringing miracle and misery. Just like it had to every previous guardian.

Should I have known better, yes? For such a young man, I already understood the yank of the earth: dropped knife, ladder down to steerage, mourning song. Of all people, I shouldn't have fallen for Golem's charms. So I flung the last piece over the rail and into the sea. It splashed and disappeared—good riddance!—only to bob back up to the surface.

Golem's face looking up at me, ever smiling. Laughing even.

The Rabbi and the Vampire

Darren Stein

I WAS NOT THERE WHEN the girl came sprinting past the darkened workshops and tanneries towards the Jüdenstraße, her feet mercifully numb as they slid and slit against the icy cobblestones beneath them. I would see her injuries later; would mop up the blood that she trailed across the floor from her ravaged soles; would tend to the scratches that had torn across her hands and arms from where he had tried to snatch her.

I could imagine her desperately weaving between the putrid reek of steaming vats, broken crates, and rusting mechanical devices like a mouse trying to escape a toying tomcat. The terror which drove her through our little gate, left half ajar and unguarded due to years of mutual conditioning from those both within and without, must have been incentive indeed. And so, her pretty blonde hair trailing in the wind, she had run to the only light she could see and crashed through the door into my grandfather's synagogue to the mirrored horror of those inside.

"Please!" she cried, coming to rest on her knees before the crowd of bearded men, who, like some pastiche from the fairy tale of Snow White and the Seven Dwarfs, stared down at this alien creature, young and beautiful and in obvious distress. They, with their yarmulkes and tzitzit, all dressed in modest black suits with only their age, height, and girth appearing to differentiate them. She, conversely, wore a white dress, its hems and arms stained with blood, wet from the freezing snow.

"Please!" she begged. "I seek sanctuary."

All eyes turned, as they naturally would on any complex question, to the Rabbi— my grandfather, who had risen from his chair at the end of a long table covered in holy books. His dark brown eyes stared at the young woman from his own worn and startled face. He stroked his long silver beard anxiously and then appeared to make a decision.

"Bring bandages, boiling water, and honey to help disinfect her wounds," he said to the men standing beside him.

"Abraham," he turned to me, "go and get your mother and sister. It is not right for us to be alone with this woman."

So begrudgingly, then only ten years old, I had run back to my home to do as my grandfather had asked. My mother, already dozing after the day's exertion, stirred uncomfortably but followed me with my sixteen-year-old sister to the synagogue. When we returned, someone had placed the girl in a chair and fetched a glass of water from which she was eagerly drinking. Levi Cohen, one of my grandfather's students, had lifted her legs upon a saddlebag and was examining the wounds beneath her feet.

"There are pieces of glass wedged between the webbing of her toes." He grimaced. "She will need to have them removed to prevent serious infection."

A pained expression crept across the girl's face. "Please," she said, addressing my grandfather, who she now recognized as a leader. "Please grant me sanctuary."

My grandfather looked at her thoughtfully, and then sat down on a chair beside her so that he could speak to her face to face. He seemed more comfortable now that my mother and sister were there. "We cannot give you sanctuary, my dear," he said, "because we have no such thing as sanctuary. Your people, I regret to say, have never recognized the sanctity of our places of worship and study. They have attacked our synagogues and yeshivas with complete disregard for their holiness, and so, I cannot offer you the protection of a place that will be recognized as off-limits to those who might wish to harm you."

The girl's eyes dropped in despair.

"What we can do," my grandfather continued, "is hide you."

The girl looked up, hopefully. "Can you? I mean, I am not sure if you can."

"Then, you will need to tell us who exactly you are fleeing from."

She gave him a fearful look and glanced around the room at the bearded faces of the congregation.

"Perhaps, gentlemen," said my grandfather to his congregants, "it would be best if you all went home. My family and I are more than able to care for this young girl."

"We thank you for thinking of our safety, Rabbi," motioned one of the elderly men, "but whatever danger she has brought into the ghetto will affect us all. There is no point trying to martyr yourself."

"Indeed." My grandfather nodded. "You are right. But perhaps we can diminish the impact of it."

The men looked at him uncertainly.

"Please," he said reassuringly, "if there are to be consequences, it would naturally be better if you were all with your families. Go home through the rear exit and say psalms for us. We will meet again for prayers in the morning."

So once again, they bowed to his wishes and shuffled off in silent conversation, looking back with concern at the young woman, and our little family gathered around her.

My mother took over the binding of her feet while my sister washed the blood from her arms, and I tried as gently as possible to bandage them with linen strips.

"I think," the young woman shivered, "it was an aristocrat."

My grandfather raised his eyebrows while my mother began to shake nervously.

"He came into the city from the castle in the mountains. He told my parents he was a relative of the Count."

My grandfather watched her apprehensively.

"I see," he said after a few moments of hesitation. "I understand you must be very frightened."

She was breathing quickly again. "I think he means to kill me. I think he wanted to...eat me."

My sister squealed and then brought her fist to her mouth out of embarrassment. My mother turned to my grandfather.

"Papa," she cried, "she cannot stay here! She is a danger to us all."

My grandfather placed his hand reassuringly on my mother's shoulder.

"I understand the nature of the situation," he said, smiling, "and I appreciate your advice. It is not without its virtue." He then turned to my sister. "Chana. Get this young lady one of your Sabbath dresses." My sister's eyes widened in horror. "I will buy you a new one."

And though my sister seemed uncomfortable with this prospect, the payoff seemed to appease her, and she hurried home to pick out one of her least favorite outfits.

I took over my sister's role as nurse and tried my best to wash and clean her wounds with a moist cloth before daubing honey over the cuts and scratches. As the girl winced at my touch, I bandaged her arms with twists of fabric, but she did not resist. Far worse was my mother's attempts to draw the splinters and glass from her savaged feet, and I could see her biting her lip in order to resist the temptation to withdraw her limbs.

When my sister returned with some clothing, my grandfather stood and ushered me towards the corner of the room. There we stood staring at the blank wall, neither speaking nor moving as the women helped her into the clean garments.

"Thank you," she said notably to my sister, who she recognized for having given up one of her dresses.

My sister smiled and nodded politely but did not speak, looking at her beautiful visage with caution.

"You have cared for the stranger," my grandfather purred. "A great mitzvah, a good deed. And now you must return home," he said earnestly.

"But Papa..." my mother tried to argue, but my grandfather raised a finger, and as always, my mother showed complete obedience.

"Try to mop up the blood with some lemon juice to hide the smell, and then hurry home. Lock the doors and do not open them until I return. You too can say psalms for me," he said, assuring her that this would be the most constructive act she could perform.

"Abraham," he then turned to me, "before you join your mother and sister, you will show this young lady the recess where you and your friends hide behind the Aron Kodesh. Help her lie comfortably and then wall the space around her with holy books before pulling back the bookshelf to conceal the opening."

I frowned as I slowly processed all that he had asked me and then directed the young girl towards the raised platform at the end of the room. The Aron Kodesh housed the holy Torah in what amounted to a curtained cupboard. Behind it was a small recess, just large enough for two adults to sit side by side. Limping and clearly, in a lot of pain, the girl struggled to crawl behind the wooden fixture, her new dress snagging on a wooden splinter and ripping her replacement clothes. Then suddenly from outside came a loud piercing screech as if from some type of animal. The girl froze in terror and looked back at my grandfather.

"You will have to hide with her, Abraham," said my grandfather earnestly. "Quickly now, and do not make a sound, no matter what you see or hear."

I pulled the bookshelves closed behind us and stacked some prayer books in front of the cracks to try and make our presence less apparent. While the girl hyperventilated in fear, I knelt down and pressed my eye against a tiny hole in the Aron Kodesh, just making out my grandfather in the hazy view it afforded.

Somehow, he did not seem frightened but rather determined. He looked towards the entrance to the synagogue and then spoke out in a loud and clear voice.

"You need not continue to wait for me to exit the building," he said. "You may enter if you so wish!"

In an instant, another presence was in the room.

"How very gracious," said a tightly clipped and sardonic voice. A tall man dressed in elegant, dark green garments stood before my grandfather. He had sharp, pale features, a black mustache, and sideburns that grew thinly across his face.

"Shalom Aleichem," said my grandfather.

The man's eyes narrowed suspiciously.

"I believe you might have something that belongs to me, Jew," said the man offhandedly as his eyes studied the room. He gazed down at the book-strewn table but appeared to be careful not to touch anything.

"Everything ultimately belongs to God," my grandfather bowed.

"Indeed," the man smiled. "Alas, it seems there is little difference between our preachers and yours."

He proceeded to pace up and down, investigating his environment while my grandfather remained impassive.

"Reality," he said, "is somewhat different. Everything ultimately belongs to those with power here on Earth."

"You seem agitated, Sir," said my grandfather with a note of pious concern.

"We both know a girl came into the ghetto," the man snapped. "I can smell her. Now hand her over, Jew!" he shouted, approaching my grandfather, but did not touch him.

The girl grabbed my arm as I watched, and I unconsciously took her hand. My grandfather, however, looked into the man's eyes.

"You have clearly not been doing this for very long," he mused, regarding the man carefully.

"Excuse me?" he growled.

"This," he motioned back and forth, referring to the two of them. "The count it seems has not instructed you about our history."

"What?" the man began to rage.

"Forgive me," my grandfather demured, "our history."

The man appeared to be confused.

"If you do not give me what I have come for, Jew, I will rip your throat open and feast on your blood!"

"You cannot touch me," said Grandfather cautiously. "No vampire can."

Up until that time, I had never heard the word "vampire." The girl next to me cringed at the sound of the word, and the man himself seemed shocked that he had been identified.

"So you know what I am?" he grinned.

"Oh, yes." My grandfather nodded. "But it seems you do not know what I am."

The vampire stared at him, appraisingly.

"If you were to ask the count, he will tell you that you cannot suck the blood of a Jew."

"And why not?" asked the vampire with curious irritation.

"Because we are a holy people, a nation of priests. As God's chosen people, we do not need symbols of faith to ward you off. We have our blood covenant. Our holiness runs through our veins, the very life force that you so desire."

"Nonsense!" The vampire laughed, but he seemed uncertain.

"Do not take my word for it," beckoned my grandfather. "I will happily give you my arm or my neck so that you may taste for yourself. But I warn you, it will be the last thing that you ever drink."

"I don't have to kill you to drink your blood, old Jew. I can simply kill you for the pleasure." He grinned widely.

"True," my grandfather agreed. "It is unfortunate that your kind has long caused difficulties for my people. The Count would drain the blood from a young Christian child and place the body at the ghetto gates. The Christians would then accuse the Jews of murdering the child and using their blood to bake our Passover Matzah. Vicious pogroms would be perpetrated against my community as a result."

"Ingenious!" The vampire smirked.

"Perhaps," my grandfather said sadly. "We have known of your kind for thousands of years. The first vampires were called Am Lak, the lickers of blood, from a tribe called the Amalekites."

A sense of recognition crossed the vampire's face. "From the Bible – the story of the Exodus," he said. "They attacked the Israelites from behind. Moses raised his hands while they fought off the attack, and whenever he lowered them, the Amalekites would win. Whenever he raised them, the Hebrews would win."

"Well done," my grandfather smiled. "You know your scripture."

"I have not always been this way." The vampire stared down at my grandfather, who had sat upon a chair. "There was something else," he said, approaching the old man. "God instructed the Israelites to kill the Amalekites. To wipe them off the face of the Earth."

"That is also true," said my grandfather. "It is a very powerful commandment, and one which, till now, I have never had the honor of fulfilling."

"What!" cried the vampire, but it was too late. My grandfather seized the vampire by the arms and from his seated position, pulled him towards him. He recited a Hebrew verse as the vampire struggled.

"I shall surely erase the memory of Amalek from under the heavens."

The vampire began to shake and scream in agony.

"God is my miracle. For the Hand is on the throne of God. God maintains a war against Amalek, from generation to generation."

As my grandfather continued, reciting the verses a total of three times, the vampire appeared to waver and collapse, his body convulsing, bubbling, thinning, and desiccating before my very eyes. When my grandfather finally stopped, there was nothing but the lavish garments that the beast had worn.

Beads of sweat peppered my grandfather's brow, and he sat, breathless. I did not dare speak or call out to him. I was frozen in awe at what I had witnessed.

As if knowing that I could see him, he raised his hand and beckoned in my direction. I pushed the shelves aside and slid out. Leaving the nervous girl behind me, I ran and fetched my grandfather a glass of water and helped him drink, his hands still shaking from the ordeal.

"Thank you, Abraham." He smiled.

I looked down at the man's clothes. "Is he really gone, Grandfather?" I asked.

My grandfather nodded. "We can only hope that the series of events that brought him here do not bring others of his kind," he said.

"Others?" I thought.

"It is perhaps time we helped to return that young girl to her family," he said. "Go and get your mother and sister, and together, we will take her back to the Christian side."

And so our little family escorted the young woman out of the ghetto to her home. My grandfather had reasoned that the city's authorities would be less likely to suspect a whole family of foul play than two males accompanying an injured woman in the early hours of the morning, irrespective of their age. Her family was indeed relieved, elated, and very grateful that their daughter had been saved from both a humiliating and deadly fate by no less than a group of Jews.

Emily Stoker, as her name turned out to be, spoke very highly of my grandfather and his role in protecting her, as well as how I had sat with her in the darkness and helped stop her from screaming or going insane when her pursuer had appeared. And so it was that some days later, her father, a wealthy industrialist, entered the ghetto and approached our little synagogue. He had a proposition for our family, a way he proposed to thank us and grant us an opportunity that we would never otherwise receive. He wished to adopt me, to take me out of the ghetto and give me a secular education—access to opportunities that I would never receive, either in the ghetto or as a Jew.

My grandfather was vehemently against it. He argued that my identity was not a matter for compromise. Yet it was my mother who stood against him. After all the years of acquiescence to his will, she stood firm on the man's offer.

"Abraham knows who he is, Papa," she cried. "He will return to us one day. And although I understand your fears for him, I can see the hope he would never otherwise have."

A few weeks later, I left the ghetto to attend schools in Berlin, then Paris, and finally Dublin, where my adoptive family established themselves after the Revolutionary outbreaks of the 1840s. Although I visited my family in the early years, I did not maintain my religious identity. As my grandfather had feared, it was all too easy to assimilate, to lose the rigidity of Jewish observance when not amongst a broader community of one's own. That was the existential danger of pulling down the ghetto walls. How would we maintain our identity when we were no longer forced to be Jews?

Although there is much that I had forgotten, I would always remember the night where I watched an old Rabbi kill a vampire with words from the holy Torah. I would never forget the one commandment that God had given to my ancestors, to kill the Amalekites, those lickers of blood. So later, when I began to write, I decided to expose these creatures for what they were, to identify their characteristics and extol their weaknesses, so that others would know them when they encountered them, and understand how to eradicate them when necessary. Although some friends have given me hope that I have been successful, the results, I believe, will be known only long after I am gone.

Bram.

Authors

CAROLYN GEDULD

Carolyn Geduld is a mental health professional in Bloomington, Indiana. Her fiction has appeared in The Writing Disorder, Pennsylvania Literary Review, Persimmon Tree, Not Your Mother's Breastmilk, Dime Store Review, Dual Coast (Prolific Press), Otherwise Engaged, and several others.

DARREN STEIN

Darren Stein is a Jewish-Australian poet and writer who teaches English, History and Studies of Religion at a high school on Sydney's North Shore. He is descended from a long-line of Jewish refugees - his German grandparents who fled the Nazis in 1937, and his Lithuanian great-grandparents who fled pogroms three decades earlier. His writing appears in regular print and he has published two anthologies, The Nut House Poems and Storage Space.

DAVID MARGOLIS

David Margolis retired from the practice of gastroenterology in 2013 to become a full time writer. His stories and poems have appeared in The Canadian Medical Association Journal, JAMA: Internal Medicine, Missouri Medicine, HumorPress.com, Long Story Short, Still Crazy, The Jewish Light of St. Louis, and the Society of Classical Poets. He's published three novels, "The Myth of Dr. Kugelman", "The Plumber's Wrench," and "The Misadventures of Buddy Jones" which won an eLit award for humor. He's also written a book of short stories, "Looking Behind: The Gaseous Life of a Gastroenterologist." "Ungodliness" was written as one of a collection of short stories with a Jewish theme. David resides in St. Louis, MO with his wife Laura, two rescue teen-agers, three small rescue dogs, and a set of golf clubs.

ELIZA MASTER

Eliza Master began writing with crayons stored in an old cookie tin. Since then, many magazines have published her stories. Eliza's three novellas, The Scarlet Cord, The Twisted Rope and The Shibari Knot are newly released by Wayzgoose Press. She attempts to make each day better than the previous one. When Eliza isn't writing you can find her amongst brightly colored clay pots dreaming of her next adventure.

HADLEY SCHERZ-SCHINDLER

Hadley Scherz-Schindler grew up in St. Louis, Missouri, a city full of music, barbeque and ghosts. She married into a family of rabbis and has four children who drift between college, grad school and home like seasonal storms. Hadley still lives in St. Louis with her husband, Josh, and their collie, Frodo.

KEN GOLDMAN

Ken Goldman, former Philadelphia teacher of English and Film Studies, is an Active member of the Horror Writers Association. His stories have appeared in over 900 independent press publications in the U.S., Canada, the UK, and Australia with over thirty due for publication in 2019. Since 1993 Ken's tales have received seven honorable mentions in The Year's Best Fantasy & Horror. He has written five books : three anthologies of short stories, YOU HAD ME AT ARRGH!! (Sam's Dot Publishers), DONNY DOESN'T LIVE HERE ANYMORE (A/A Productions) and STAR-CROSSED (Vampires 2); and a novella, DESIREE, (Damnation Books).

His first novel OF A FEATHER (Horrific Tales Publishing) was released in January 2014. SINKHOLE, his second novel, was published by Bloodshot Books August 2017.

Lorraine Schein

Lorraine Schein is the child of two Holocaust survivors who met in NYC. Her work has appeared in VICE Terraform, Strange Horizons, Syntax & Salt, and Little Blue Marble, and in the anthologies Tragedy Queens: Stories Inspired by Lana del Rey & Sylvia Plath, and Spectral Lines. The Futurist's Mistress, her poetry book, is available from mayapplepress.com.

MARC MORGENSTERN

Marc Morgenstern is a recent graduate of the Warren Wilson College MFA Program for Writers and just completed his first short story collection. Marc has begun work on a novel and currently volunteers as an associate teacher for the UCLA Wordcommandos, a creative writing workshop for veterans with PTSD. In 2019, his story about a young cantor and his wife was featured by the New Short Fiction Series, Los Angeles' longest-running spoken word production. Marc's essays and articles have appeared in The New York Times, Huffington Post, The Christian Science Monitor and Child magazine. He's worked as a professional print journalist for the Washington Post Company and was an Emmy-winning TV News Producer for the CBS TV Stations. Marc lives in Santa Monica, CA.

YAEL LEVY

Yael Levy writes contemporary Middle Grade and Young Adult books, graphic novels, and screenplays based on Jewish history, folklore and mythology. A native New Yorker and Atlanta transplant, Yael currently lives in the hills of Jerusalem. He find more at website yaellevyauthor.com.

About the Publisher

Madness Heart Press is dedicated to bringing you quality horror from new and amazing authors. You can find more books, stories and even listen to the Madness Heart Radio Podcast at MadnessHeart.Press

Made in the USA
Lexington, KY
10 December 2019